SALINE DISTRICT LIBRARY

P9-CRD-188

Mystery Bow
Bowen, Peter
Long son

LONG
SON

ALSO BY PETER BOWEN

Thunder Horse
Notches
Wolf, No Wolf
Specimen Song
Coyote Wind

Imperial Kelly
Kelly Blue
Yellowstone Kelly

LONG
SON

A GABRIEL DU PRÉ MYSTERY

Peter Bowen

St. Martin's Press
New York

APR 1999

SALINE DISTRICT LIBRARY
Saline, Michigan 48176

LONG SON. Copyright © 1999 by Peter Bowen. All rights reserved. Printed in the United States of America. No part of this book may be used or reproduced in any manner whatsoever without written permission except in the case of brief quotations embodied in critical articles or reviews. For information address St. Martin's Press, 175 Fifth Avenue, New York, N.Y. 10010.

Library of Congress Cataloging-in-Publication Data

Bowen, Peter.
    Long son / Peter Bowen.
       p.   cm.
    ISBN 0-312-19917-1
    I. Title.
    PS3552.O866L66   1999
    813'.54—dc21   98-48954
                                  CIP

First Edition: April 1999

10 9 8 7 6 5 4 3 2 1

For David and Sarah

LONG SON

✤ CHAPTER 1 ✤

Du Pré and Madelaine stood at the back of the crowd. The auctioneer rattled the bid and the carved walnut sideboard went for fourteen hundred dollars. The buyer was a cold-eyed woman in designer expedition gear. Her Mercedes-Benz SUV had Bozeman license plates. The sideboard would go to her store and grow greatly in price.

A couple college kids backed a rental truck around and they put the sideboard in the back.

It was a raw March day with snow promised in the wind's scent.

The auctioneer offered three more pieces of furniture, and they all went to the woman from Bozeman, too. The college boys loaded the pieces and they slid down the door and locked it and got in and drove off. The woman was counting out hundred-dollar bills to the lawyer who was taking the cash and checks.

"It is very sad," said Madelaine, "I don't know the Messmers but they are here a long time and this place is gone, too."

One more old family ranch ended, five or six generations of people who had made a living here, working in the wind.

The Messmer place was west of Toussaint forty miles. The Wolf Mountains shoved storms right at it. The weather was rough but the weather brought water.

The Messmers had bought a motor home, to go south for the cold months. They went. Down on the border the motor home

1

blew a front tire and the top-heavy vehicle went over. Mr. and Mrs. Messmer both died.

"They have a daughter, eh?" said Madelaine. "She is killed but they never find out who?"

Du Pré nodded.

She is found along the highway, behind a gravel pile put there by the Highway Department, one bullet in her head. Bullet blows up in her head, Du Pré remembered, little pieces, can't even tell what it was. Nothing. Nobody caught.

Long time gone, 1980, '82, something like that.

"They have son, too," said Du Pré. "Bad kid. He is in some trouble, he is sent away, he don't come back here. I don't know what happen, him. I think he is sent to that Boy's Town or something."

Beat a horse to death, that was it, rope the horse up it can't move and beat its head in, a sledgehammer. Mean little shit, Catfoot tell me about it.

Du Pré looked over at the farm machinery ranked in rows. All you needed to raise wheat. Big tractors, plows, drills, sprayers, even a combine. Pretty good ranch afford its own combine. Most people they contract it out.

Nothing for that hay, though, they are not selling the cutters and rakes and balers.

Du Pré looked off toward the old white ranch house. The house was shabby, paint peeling, shingles mangy. On a ranch the animals and equipment usually had better buildings than the people who owned them.

A man came out of the house. He was about forty, dark, six feet tall. He wore a three-piece suit and irrigation boots. No hat. Dark glasses.

"That is him?" said Madelaine.

Du Pré couldn't remember what the mean little shit looked like, or if he had ever seen him.

Catfoot and Mama they are killed 1983, Catfoot is drunk, the train hit them.

Son of a bitch, life, just like that.

Du Pré shrugged.

"We get somethin' to eat," said Madelaine, "They auction the china and stuff after the guns and the tools. That take an hour maybe."

Du Pré nodded. They walked back to his old cruiser and got in and Madelaine took some sandwiches out of a cooler in the back seat and a plastic tub of the good crabapple sauce she made. They ate. Madelaine had some pink wine and Du Pré sipped whiskey and they smoked, the big handrolled cigarettes for after eating. Handrolling meant you could build the smoke the size you wanted.

"This guy he maybe come back and run this ranch?" said Madelaine.

Du Pré shrugged.

"I hate it when them places go," said Madelaine, "All the stories are gone, too."

My Madelaine, Du Pré thought, she got this cheap old oak table maybe cost three dollars, Sears & Roebuck, hundred years ago, she love that table. Got burns on it, some drunk carve his initials in it, she love that table.

Think, Du Pré she say, all the things got said around this table.

Old piece of shit, I spend about two weeks fixing it, so it don't fall to splinters.

"My oak table is not a piece of shit, Du Pré," said Madelaine.

Du Pré looked at her.

"You thinking pret' loud there," said Madelaine. "We go now, maybe buy that china."

Madelaine had her heart set on some gold-rimmed flowered china that she said was old and very valuable.

I pay for it, I eat off of it, I don't care, Du Pré thought.

When the china set finally came up for bids Du Pré got the whole set, minus a few broken over the decades, for eighty dollars. He paid the lawyer the money and then he picked up two boxes and Madelaine the third and they walked back to the old cruiser and slid them into the back seat.

"Anything else you want?" said Du Pré.

Madelaine shook her head.

Du Pré got in the car.

"Where you know, this china?" he said.

"Susan Klein hear about it think I maybe like it," said Madelaine.

Women, Du Pré thought, know about everything.

He started the car. He turned around and he headed down the long drive toward the bench road.

A couple of hands were hazing some cows toward the barn. The cows were huge in the belly and ready to calve.

"Bet you are glad you don't do that no more," said Madelaine.

"Yah," said Du Pré. Pulling calves was hard work, and it usually went on day and night for weeks. He'd been kicked once so hard his left femur snapped and he heard it break, like a stick on a knee.

They got close to the gate and the cattle guard. Du Pré looked over. There was a cow there already calving, and the calf's rear legs were out. It was stuck. The cow bawled in pain.

Du Pré backed up until he could turn around and he drove up to the ranch buildings. The hands were moving the cows very slowly. Du Pré went through the fence and trotted toward the riders.

A cow lay dead in a little hollow.

Blood seeped from a hole in her skull. She had a live calf part-way out, too.

Du Pré stopped and waited. He waved at the riders.

They didn't move any faster and it was ten minutes before the lead rider got to him.

The man was an ordinary hand, middle-aged, weathered, bent. His face was dark with sun and his clothes filthy.

"You got a cow in trouble, the gate," said Du Pré.

The hand nodded.

"Thanks," he said, "I knew that."

Du Pré looked at him. That cow was a lot of money and her calf would die soon without help.

The hand looked at him.

"The boss said do the easy ones and shoot the others."

Du Pré looked at him.

"He's gettin' out of the cow business," said the hand. "It don't make any sense to me either."

"Who is your boss?" asked Du Pré.

"That son of a bitch Larry Messmer," said the hand. "I worked here ten years for his folks. Soon as the calves are in, we get paid off. Got to be gone by the end of the month."

Du Pré shook his head.

"Say, mister," said the hand, "you know anybody lookin' for good hands?"

Du Pré shook his head.

There were very few jobs anymore in the cattle country.

The hand looked past Du Pré. He put heels to his horse and trotted after the cows and his partner.

Du Pré turned.

Larry Messmer was standing at the fence, feet apart, looking out at Du Pré.

Du Pré waved.

5

Messmer didn't take his hands out of his pockets.

Messmer was looking at something far away.

Du Pré walked back to the fence and stepped through and he went to his car and got in.

"It is him," said Du Pré, "that Larry Messmer."

"What is with his cows?" said Madelaine.

Du Pré shook his head and started the engine.

❧ CHAPTER 2 ❧

Raymond, Du Pré's son-in-law, lay in the bed. His left leg was in plaster and held up by a wire and pulley and weight. He had a bandage around his head and his left arm was in a cast, too. Tubes from plastic bags on poles ran to his arm.

"Raymond!" said Jacqueline. "Oh, you are hurt!" She leaned over and hugged him.

Du Pré had driven her down to Billings. Raymond had fallen eighty feet from a scaffold, landing on his side, in soft earth, but for the rocks, three, which hadn't been so soft. The one his head hit was a few inches under the soil, or he would have been dead.

His entire face was purple and his lips were so swollen they looked like big chunks of raw liver.

Jacqueline was careful not to touch him hard. He bubbled a few words.

"You are sorry!" said Jacqueline. "Big fool, you think I think you do this for fun? I am happy you are alive."

She leaned over and she put her ear to his lips.

"Of course he do that," she said.

Of course I go inspect the damn brands, Du Pré thought, there is no one else do it, me.

Back to the cow-ass business. Boring. One cow ass is not like another but telling them apart is boring, if I can still do it.

"Madelaine is watching the kids," said Jacqueline. "I stay here till you are better, I got a room, the motel down the street."

She leaned over to listen again.

"She handle them fine," said Jacqueline, "Madelaine is ver' tough."

Raymond bubbled.

He is laughing, Du Pré thought, well, that is good.

Father of twelve. Fourteen?

Du Pré couldn't remember how many fine grandchildren his daughter had presented him with. A big damn litter.

"You stay, Raymond," said Jacqueline, "I go and talk to the doctor."

She went off quickly.

Raymond had his eyes closed.

Du Pré sat in a chair and he looked at the magazines, all of them old and none of them at all interesting.

Raymond had been working on a grain elevator when the wind came up and the scaffold rocked and he had fallen.

Lucky. He is ver' lucky.

Busted all to shit but he is alive.

Du Pré wandered out of the room looking for a place to smoke but there were signs every ten feet promising death to those who lit up. He finally took the elevator down to the first floor and went out the front entrance and rolled a smoke and lit it. He nodded at the hospital staff who were smoking, too.

Du Pré grinned.

A couple men in blue scrubs grinned back.

"You are doctors?" said Du Pré.

They nodded.

"Good," said Du Pré.

He finished his smoke and went back up to the room. Jacqueline was still gone. Du Pré looked at Raymond. He seemed to be sleeping. Little bubbles formed on his lips.

Jacqueline bustled in ahead of a physician, a big, heavy, white-haired man whose lab coat was buttoned wrong.

"He say Raymond be here maybe a month," said Jacqueline. "He is bad broke up. His brain is okay, though."

"His brain is okay, how come I got twelve grandkids?" said Du Pré.

"Not his brain, give you those grandkids," said Jacqueline. "Last twins, they tie my tubes, so you can remember, Papa, there are thirteen grandchildren."

Du Pré nodded.

"Thirteen," said the doctor, "and he's twenty-seven? My, my."

"He don't do much," said Jacqueline. "Me, I do most of the work, you know."

"Remarkable," said the doctor, "very remarkable. Now, we need to keep him a while to make sure he hasn't got any complications and he does have multiple bad fractures. Leg, ribs, arm, wrist, skull—and he may have to have some surgery. He's in good shape, though, considering."

"You can go back, Papa," said Jacqueline, "Raymond he sleep a lot, and I stay here. I get a cab to the motel, my bags."

Du Pré nodded.

He hated hospitals. The smell. His wife had died in one.

That is the day I want to find God, kick His Teeth down His Throat.

God, He is scarce a while, me.

Jacqueline hugged Du Pré. He kissed her.

"You got money?" he asked.

"Yah," she said.

"I send more you need it."

"Okay," said Jacqueline. "You help Madelaine, my kids, Papa."

Du Pré made a face.

9

Jacqueline punched him in the arm.

"Be good," she said, "or I adopt another twelve, fifteen."

The doctor laughed.

Du Pré went out and down the stairs and out the front door to the parking lot. He got in his old cruiser and reached under the seat for the bottle of whiskey and had a gulp. He put the bottle back and started the car, went down the trunk road to the interstate and east until he came to the north highway and he went off the exit and around and he gunned the engine.

Go eighty on the freeway, two-lane it is a hundred and ten, he thought, lots of them Highway Patrol on the freeway.

It was early afternoon. He and Jacqueline had left right after Raymond had been taken out in the helicopter. It was a six- or seven-hour drive from Cooper to Billings at sixty-five. Du Pré made it in four hours.

The road stretched straight as a string north over the rolling High Plains.

There were fat gray clouds off east moving toward the west. Storms from the east were always bad. The clouds were blizzard-colored.

Du Pré looked at them.

I will be home an hour before it hits, he thought.

He went around a semi pulling two trailers. The driver blew a blast on his air horn.

There was still snow piled in the draws and coulees where the wind had drifted it over the winter. Sometimes sixty feet deep. When the snow finally melted, there would be dead deer in the tops of the trees. They had wandered out on the snow and sank and died.

Du Pré hit a pool of water at the bottom of a hill and spray shot out seventy feet on either side of the cruiser, knocking a meadowlark off a fencepost.

He slowed at the top of the next long hill. If there was anything just over the top going slowly, he needed to be doing only fifty if he wanted to stop in time.

The hill's shield dropped and Du Pré saw open road and floored the accelerator.

From the top of one hill to the top of the next one was fifteen miles. One car far up ahead.

Du Pré roared on.

Canada geese in a long vee flew west, looking for a lake to weather the blizzard in.

March storms could drop five feet of wet heavy snow, choke the rivers with slush that jelled to dams and send water spilling over the plains.

Mean damn country, I love it.

Du Pré passed the car, a new one, the driver's face a white and frightened blur as Du Pré shot past.

He braked before the hilltop, crested, looked down, and gunned the engine.

Drive sane you never get anywhere.

Du Pré saw the Highway Patrol car too late. It was hidden behind a row of poplars a long-gone homesteader had put up to cut the wind.

Du Pré looked in the rearview mirror. The cop car wallowed out on the road and the light bar flashed on.

Du Pré turned on his light bar.

The patrolman shut his off and slowed down.

Ah, Du Pré thought, it is good to be a half-drunk brand inspector with this fine car, got flashing lights. No siren. I don't turn the radio on either.

The storm was moving fast.

Du Pré pulled up to the Toussaint Saloon just as the wind had picked up and the first wet white clumps of snow splatted.

He parked and went in.

"Hi," said Susan Klein. She was smiling a little too much.

She made a tall highball for Du Pré, whiskey ditch.

She pushed it over.

"Two of these," she said, "and you get on over to Raymond and Jackie's to help Madelaine."

Du Pré grimaced.

"Two," said Susan Klein, "I'll give you a bottle to go. But you ain't getting snowed in here and leaving her with those kids."

Du Pré looked sad.

"You cowardly son of a bitch," said Susan Klein.

"Three," said Du Pré.

"No way," said Susan Klein.

Damn women, Du Pré thought, they got a union.

✤ CHAPTER 3 ✤

G et rid of mine, look what happens," said Madelaine, "God He is some pissant, got a great sense of humor."

"Very," said Father Van Den Heuvel. The big priest sat at the kitchen table, before him a big cup of tea with brandy in it. He dropped small cups and probably would drop this one, too. But it was plastic and not china.

"Thirteen of them," said Du Pré. "Me, I thought there was twelve."

"Twelve, Jackie and Raymond's," said Madelaine. "Then Jacqueline find this orphan, a powwow, bring her home. Sweet little girl she is four."

"Jesus," said Du Pré, "that is maybe kidnapping."

"No," said Madelaine. "Jackie call her mother, get her grandmother, mother is in jail, grandmother has a stroke, can't move hardly, she say please take the kid."

"Did anyone," asked Father Van Den Heuvel, "um, ah, do any paperwork about this?"

"Kid can't eat paperwork, paperwork don't keep her clean, a warm bed," said Madelaine. "She is thin, got those head lice, now she is plump and happy. Paperwork."

Father Van Den Heuvel nodded. He knew better than to ramble on.

"Me, I don't notice," said Du Pré.

"You are so full of shit, Du Pré," said Madelaine. "I see you look, those kids, you know everything about them. You think you are a grump they don't bother you. They are kids, they know you are full of shit. Kids know, them things."

There was a reasonably destructive riot going on in the children's wing of the house, where Jacqueline and Raymond had put in double bunks and plastic windows and a tough linoleum floor. The walls were once white and now mostly various crayons' colors.

"I go see I quiet them down," said Madelaine. She walked off, her hips swaying.

The noise quit.

Then it started again, one voice louder than all the others. Madelaine's. A pillow fight. There were also toy tubes of foam with which a kid could beat on another kid without damage.

Soft thumps.

Shrieks.

"Yahooooooooooooooo!" yelled Madelaine.

The riot notched up.

"Those are fortunate children," said the big priest, "they are loved."

Du Pré grunted.

Little bastards drive me nuts, the boys get a little older, it is the last time I get to hunt my own self, this life. Fish, either.

Du Pré hated fishing. It bored him, the fish stank, and he didn't like eating them.

I fish a bunch, too. Fun.

Madelaine came back, pink and flushed and beautiful.

"Boys got a fort, the far end," she said, "us girls charge them, run them out, count a lot of coup."

The riot stopped.

"They are tired now," said Madelaine. "Another fifteen minutes, time for prayers and bed."

14

Father Van Den Heuvel beamed.

"What you so happy about?" asked Madelaine. "They got an altar in there, they pray to the Muppets."

The big priest turned his hands palms up to the ceiling.

"Heaven," said Madelaine, "is full of Muppets, you are that age."

"And the Cookie Monster is in hell?" said the priest.

"No hell," said Madelaine. "Who needs hell?"

Van Den Heuvel grinned. He was in this remote posting because while teaching in seminary, he remarked to an entire class of would-be priests that the Bible was a wonderful piece of literature, and no more than that. His superiors wished it was still possible to burn heretics at the stake, but it wasn't, so they sent Father Van Den Heuvel to deepest Montana. He loved it, and when asked by his superiors if he had had a spiritual awakening and therefore a better take on the Testaments he always assured them he had not, and that further, heaven was full of Muppets.

They left him alone after that.

His small congregation had a lot of Métis in it, and Métis are gamblers, and so each and every Sunday serious money, for Métis, was laid on whether or not the big priest would slam his head in the door of his car and miss the services due to unconsciousness, or drop the salver or chalice, or fall off the pulpit, or down the steps leading to the altar.

His one attempt at cutting his own firewood had led to a hundred or so stitches. He tried to relight his furnace once and it blew up and burned down his tiny house, so the congregation had to build him a new one.

Father Van Den Heuvel loved and cared for his flock and they him.

The last priest had been an alcoholic prick, always bitching about something or other.

15

Father Van Den Heuvel was gentle and kind and never judged.

"You tell them a story," said Madelaine, looking at Du Pré.

Du Pré shrugged.

"They want their grand-père to tell them a story," said Madelaine. "They like your stories."

Du Pré nodded.

Now I got to make up another goddamn story and I am tired.

"A nice Bible story?" said Father Van Den Heuvel. His watery blue eyes twinkled.

"Bible stories aren't too nice," said Madelaine. "They are meant to scare the shit out of people."

Van Den Heuvel nodded.

"There are a couple . . ." he said.

"Go tell them one," said Madelaine. "They throw things they don't like it. Go on, you."

Father Van Den Heuvel shook his head.

Du Pré had some more whiskey.

My grand-père he smell of tobacco, woodsmoke, old man, whiskey, and horses.

Me, I got three of them, anyway.

Du Pré grinned thinking about Catfoot's father, who was a carver of wood and stone, who made pipes and long flutes and little animals. I see an animal, this pine knot, he would say, and then he would dig the little animal out with his knife.

Got to let this buffalo out, he would say.

Got to let out this frog.

Snake.

Bird.

The kids started to whistle and some of them stomped their feet on the floor, if they had the lower bunks.

"Ah," said Madelaine, "they want that story now."

Du Pré sighed and smoked another cigarette while the

whistling went on. Then he got up and went down the hall to the kids' room.

"Grand-père!" they yelled, and bounced on their beds. They all had their pajamas on and they all grinned to show they had brushed their teeth.

The littlest ones sat next to older brothers and sisters.

Solemn as little owls.

Du Pré looked stern.

"You have washed your faces?"

Yes.

"You brushed your teeth?"

Yes.

"Okay," said Du Pré, "I tell you a story."

The children were very respectful and quiet.

Pretty much, only giggling.

Du Pré said, I tell you why the buffalo got such big shoulders.

Long time ago . . . animals are down under the earth . . . then the time comes that they got to come up, the Grandmothers and Grandfathers who make everything say.

So the Great Bear leads all the animals, all the six-leggeds and four-leggeds and two-leggeds, except people who have to come later. Snakes wiggle along, frogs hopping, then all the animals come to the mouth of the cave and they can see a little light out there, but there is this big boulder in the way.

Great Bear he roars and shoves, but he can't do it, not even with other Great Bears, not enough of them.

There are a lot of buffalo, they are shaped like deer, tall and skinny.

The buffalo dance and there are a lot of them and then they put their foreheads to the boulder and they paw the earth and push, but they don't do nothing either, the big rock.

They need some medicine.

Coyotes pray.

Grandmothers and Grandfathers hear the prayer.

The buffalo dance and they put their foreheads to the boulder and they shove and they grow, they grow four times as big as they were and they grow huge shoulders, and they bellow and shove and the rock moves and everybody goes out into the world.

Du Pré did a little buffalo dance. He snorted and pushed.

He kissed each of his grandchildren good-night. He went out and he shut the door.

"Is that a Cree story?" asked Father Van Den Heuvel.

Du Pré looked at him.

"I am some Cree," he said, "so I guess that story is, too."

"I got hot scones," said Madelaine. "You come and eat."

❧ CHAPTER 4 ❧

Ten thousand acres. Eight, nine hundred in hay.

Du Pré looked at the cattle milling around in the big pasture. They were thirsty and the stock tank was too small to water them all.

The snow that had fallen a few days before was slumped and melting off. It was thirty degrees at eight in the morning.

Twenty stock haulers were lined up down the long drive. It would have been a lot easier to load them in smaller bunches, but Larry Messmer wanted them gone.

Du Pré shook his head. The market was down and it made no sense. Everything was to be shipped. Even unbranded calves so new they were barely able to walk.

Messmer had hired a crew who brought portable green pipe fence in sections on flatbed trucks. They assembled the corrals around the cattle.

Whole place is bassackwards, Du Pré thought.

He stood by the chute with his clipboard. The hands prodded the cattle with electric batons and they jiggled tin cans on strings at the end of poles.

The cattle rushed up the ramp into the big aluminum hauler.

Du Pré looked at brands. The calves would probably be crushed by the cattle when the hauler went around curves.

Where is that animal-rights bunch we need them?

On the sidewalk in front of pet stores, shouting slogans, drinking expensive coffee from Styrofoam cups. Near some good place, have lunch, vegetables.

The cattle streamed up the chute.

Du Pré tallied, glanced at the brands.

The Messmers had good, clear brands on most, sometimes not burned quite deep enough and haired over, but you could tell.

The only other sale this big Du Pré had inspected was an IRS sale of cattle, a corporate ranch two hundred miles away. The regular inspector had been shot and wounded.

Wife have enough of his crap, whip out her .357; fortunately she is upset and not so good a shot. He is back inspecting cattle and she is in Billings, this place they got, rude ladies.

Inspector he goes, sees her, once a week.

Blam blam blam, marriage it is saved.

Moooooooooo. Bawwwlllllllllllllll.

Cows don't got much of an act.

The cattle ran up the chutes and the hauler was filled and driven off, and another came and Du Pré tallied, and nothing at all was out of the ordinary.

Except thousands and thousands of dollars pissed away for not one good reason Du Pré could think of.

Larry Messmer stood in his three-piece suit and rubber boots, his face flat and his dead blue eyes staring.

Du Pré detested Messmer. The man was cruel.

Don't care about nothin', that one.

The cattle never stopped and neither did Du Pré.

The last hauler was loaded about four-thirty in the afternoon.

Du Pré shoved his paperwork in his leather bag and he walked off to his old cruiser.

Messmer was still standing there.

When Du Pré drove off he looked in the rearview mirror and

Messmer was speaking to a couple of men in expensive English waxed-cotton coats. Dark glasses. Fat city faces.

Shitheads.

Cows end up meat on the table, but you don't got to treat them bad.

Another goddamn day of it tomorrow and then he got no cows left. His people raise cattle, a hundred years there, gone, just like that.

Son of a bitch.

The last hauler loaded was wallowing up a muddy hill, the diesel smoke black and stinking, the heavily loaded trailer swaying.

Ammonia.

Scared cows.

Shipped to a big ranch near Sidney, near North Dakota.

No ranch rep at the loading.

Strange, such a big sale.

Whole business is strange.

Son of a bitch.

March, the dead month. Deer in the barrow pits, died of starvation just before the grass comes up, die after it comes up, new and green in spring, got no more food in it than lettuce.

The snows were melting off, even in the coulees, winter kill weathering out of the dirty drifts.

Du Pré glanced off to his left. A pair of golden eagles were gorging on dead deer meat.

Eat so much, they can't fly.

The cattle hauler wallowed. No place for Du Pré to pass.

Du Pré rolled a smoke.

I am a kid, I am in the mountains, winter, still deep winter up there, March. Catfoot's trapline. I find three martens, wire snares, dead, frozen, eyes blue with frost.

Pelt them out. It is late. I head back down, long skis, snowshoes on my back, pack, pelts, little food, sleeping bag.

See something in a meadow.

Deer stumbling in the snow, golden eagle on the deer's back, talons sunk in the deer, wings flapping, wear the deer out; it dies.

Couple coyotes waiting, walking alongside.

Eagle wear out the deer, coyotes kill it, everybody eats.

Young and strong live, get weak, get eaten.

Up there, the mountains.

The cattle hauler wallowed up to the crest of the hill. The driver stopped, an arm waved.

Du Pré slopped past.

He waved as he went down the hill toward the pond at the bottom.

The cattle hauler blew his horn.

Ain't this some shit way, run an airline?

Du Pré fished the whiskey out from under the seat and had some and set the bottle in the holder on the transom. He rolled a smoke. The light would last a while.

Cooper sat below the bench he was on. County seat, got four whole stores in it. Grocery. Feed and grain and seed, elevators to rent. Gas and bulk fuel. Bar.

Pretty good-size school, kids come, forty miles away. Spend an hour, two hours on the bus, some.

Most drive. See over the dash, drive. Twelve, maybe.

Du Pré had been driving for four years before he was old enough to get a driver's license.

He turned down the steep road that led into Cooper.

He went through the long block that was downtown and pulled up in front of the Cooper Bar. The bar was in an old bank building, next to an old school.

The old school was the County Museum.

Old photographs, dusty animal heads, saddles, blacksmith's tools, harness, a few old rifles, shotguns, faded old clothes, framed pages from the *Cooper Courier*.

Damn place even had a newspaper. Five, six hundred people, stores, houses.

Everything pretty much built without foundations, so the wind took abandoned buildings pretty quick. A few silvered boards in the long grass, all that was left of someone's dream.

Du Pré parked in front of the bar and went in. The woman behind the bar waved. She was in her fifties, blond, frog-throated from years of smoking, booze, bad marriages, toughness.

Velma.

Du Pré nodded.

"Mr. Du Pré," said Velma, "whiskey ditch?"

Du Pré hadn't been in the bar in five years but she remembered.

He put a five-dollar bill on the bar.

Velma put his drink down, a strong one, brown with the clear ice glinting.

"That museum," said Du Pré, "it is open some."

"Open now, you want the key?" said Velma.

Du Pré nodded.

Velma handed him the key, wired to a flat board a foot long.

Du Pré nodded and he walked out and left the change. It would be there when he came back.

The key turned hard in the lock. Du Pré pushed, the door was stuck. He kicked the base and it swung open.

Du Pré switched on the lights.

A big table in the center of the room held the pieces of a quilt. Mice scattered.

Quilting party is over for the winter, hasn't started again.

Du Pré saw what he had come for.

23

An old portrait of a rancher, taken in a studio in Miles City, by L. A. Huffman.

Small-brimmed Stetson, frock coat, white shirt, silk vest, black pants, and clumsy square-toed dress boots.

Big thick gold chain, turnip watch.

Pale gray eyes, a drooping thick moustache.

Du Pré looked at Larry Messmer, dead a hundred years and buried under the biggest stone in the Cooper cemetery.

❧ CHAPTER 5 ❧

She'll be right down," said Velma. "Since she retired from teaching she's lonely as hell for someone to explain things to."

Du Pré laughed.

"I'se in her little school, long before they stuck all them small schools together," said Velma. "She was young then, come out of some fancy place out East. Never married. Taught about everybody in the county."

You like to explain her, me, Du Pré thought, where the fuck you think I go to school?

Right here, Cooper, drive my old truck, high school, have Miss Porterfield for English. She don't help much, but it is not her fault.

C grades she give me, but she tells me I fiddle good even then.

I fiddle like shit then, but she is a good liar and I need one.

Du Pré sipped his drink. He had a few potato chips.

Madelaine kill me I am late, but it is so nice, quiet here, next to Raymond, Jacqueline's little monsters.

Thirteen of them. Maybe I ear-tag them, tell them apart.

"Gabriel!" said Miss Porterfield. She bustled through the front door, small, round, gray-haired, smiling. Wire-rimmed glasses. Stout woolen clothing. Irrigation boots.

"Miss Porterfield," said Du Pré, "it is good you come. I thank you."

"So you want to know about Albert Messmer?" she said.

Du Pré nodded.

Miss Porterfield slipped up on a stool next to Du Pré and she set a brown cardboard folder on the bartop.

Velma was warming a brandy snifter. She put a triple shot of brandy in it and set it next to Miss Porterfield's folder and scratched something on a tab.

"Well," said Miss Porterfield, "you've surely done well. I so like it when my students turn out. Some, alas, have ended up in Deer Lodge."

Du Pré nodded.

Big success, me, on the cover, magazines.

"Could I have one of those?" said Miss Porterfield. She nodded at Du Pré's cigarette.

Du Pré rolled her one and lit it with the shepherd's lighter his daughter Maria had sent him from Spain.

Miss Porterfield took a healthy swallow of hot brandy and she drew deep on her cigarette.

Du Pré laughed inside.

Dear old lady.

"Albert was a bastard," said Miss Porterfield. "He stole, and he was accused but not convicted of murder. Three times. The last case was that of a family who wouldn't sell their homestead to him. Their house caught fire and they were all killed. It was suspicious. Before he died, a man who had worked as Albert Messmer's foreman confessed to helping him tie the family up. The ropes burned away in the fire, of course. But Messmer was long dead by then, so it was just a story."

Miss Porterfield took another swallow of brandy. She smoked for a minute.

"But I was ahead of myself," she said, "so let me tell you of him in some more useful form . . ."

Messmer had been born in Hamburg, Germany, in 1849, and

his parents came to America and settled in Minneapolis. His father was a carpenter and his mother a laundress. Albert ran away from home in 1861, aged twelve, like so many young men. A twelve-year-old could be a cook's helper on a wagon train or cattle drive, a cabin boy on a steamship, a powder monkey setting off charges, a lot of things. More young men left home at twelve than didn't. It was a hard life then.

By 1864 Albert was in the Idaho gold fields. He was banished from one camp for stealing, another for lewd conduct. He came to Montana in 1865, to the Alder Gulch diggings, and then he disappeared for a few years, finally surfacing in Fort Benton, the head of navigation on the Missouri, in 1874. He had money and he bought a saloon and gambling hall, and men died in it from time to time. The playing cards discarded by cowboys and rivermen and card sharps and buffalo hunters were so thick on the boardwalks people slipped and fell on the slippery carpet.

When the Indians were wiped from the range in 1877, Albert Messmer staked a homestead to the west of the Wolf Mountains, south of the part of the range that was so worn they were just hills. He was married by then, and his wife filed a claim and each hand did, too, and there were a lot of hands, most of them drifters who filled out the papers for a small payment and then signed over the rights to Albert, postdated five years so as to square, at least on paper, with the law.

Albert Messmer made whiskey, sold whiskey to the Indians to the east, killing many of them, for he used strychnine in it, for kicks. His cows all seemed to bear twins and triplets.

One foreman was found dead, a gunshot wound to the temple, lying in a creekbed.

The coroner ruled it a suicide. The coroner's name was Albert Messmer. A year later he was elected to the Territorial Legislature.

Homesteaders were surrounded by Albert Messmer's ranch

holdings, and one by one they sold off, except for the family who died in the fire. There were no heirs, so Messmer got their holding, too, a good one with four big springs on it and flat, rich soil by the creek, good for hay.

After 1887, when Messmer had consolidated his holdings, there were no more rumors about him.

"He seemed to know exactly what he wanted," said Miss Porterfield, "And when he got it he quit murdering and stealing. Truthfully, it is not that unusual a story here. Very few of the Great Ancestors of the big ranchers bear up well under scrutiny."

"How he get away with all that stuff?" asked Du Pré.

"Same way people get away with it now," said Miss Porterfield. "He had money. He could buy politicians, buy silence, land—he was a little unusual, though, in that when he had what he wanted, he stopped. Most men like that never seem to get enough."

I know them people, Du Pré thought, more they get the less they have.

"One other thing," said Miss Porterfield.

Du Pré waited. Miss Porterfield had a good sense of drama and years of teaching, where one needs that.

"He had two families," said Miss Porterfield.

Du Pré chuckled.

"Like so many other men," said Miss Porterfield, "he married an Indian woman, Genevette, and they had four children. Eliza died in the early 1870s, but the children were with Messmer when he came here. Two boys, two girls. He married a white woman and the half-breed kids disappeared from view."

Du Pré nodded.

They are Métis, we take them in, sure.

Messmer had six children with his white wife, and their descendants lived and worked the Messmer ranch, right up to the sixth generation, Larry Messmer.

"I had him in school, too," said Miss Porterfield. "He was a mean, cruel little boy. And very clever. It was hard to catch him and impossible to get him to admit to anything. We had a rabbit which was found dead; it had a broken neck. And there were fires."

Du Pré nodded.

"Isn't it terrible about the Messmers?" said Miss Porterfield. "They were such fine people, they tried so hard with Larry and Janet. Janet murdered, Larry away at some awful place for bad boys. They finally buy the motor home, and get away from the winter, and . . . just like that they are dead. It's so sudden. They gave so much to the museum."

Du Pré waited.

"They were terrified of Larry," said Miss Porterfield. "They never said much, but I mentioned his name once and they looked at each other for just a moment and then they were their cheerful selves again. But they were afraid, I could see it."

Something in that bastard never is hooked up, Du Pré thought.

Him, he got them dead eyes.

"Strange they never cut him out of the will," said Miss Porterfield.

Du Pré sipped his whiskey.

"They talked about it, though."

Du Pré looked at her.

"They were thinking of donating the ranch to the Nature Conservancy," said Miss Porterfield, "not that the ranch was especially interesting, but it could be traded for something that was."

Du Pré nodded.

"Not a very nice story," said Miss Porterfield. She looked at her snifter and Velma filled it again.

Du Pré stood up.

"I got to go, herd all my grandkids," he said.

"Yes," said Miss Porterfield. "Well, bring them to the museum!"

Du Pré nodded.

You have pile of sticks, busted glass, those little bastards.

Du Pré touched his hat.

Miss Porterfield's eyes were watering.

Du Pré left before she started to cry.

✤ CHAPTER 6 ✤

D u Pré looked down the length of the trestle table at all the little maws attacking food. Tonight the victim was spaghetti, with elk balls.

I drop that poor son of a bitch of an elk, the table there, they eat him raw, Du Pré thought, I don't no longer got doubts people were cannibals. Recently.

The kids were happy and stuffing food in their faces and their table manners while not elegant at least kept food off one another's clothes.

"Salad!" said Madelaine, "You got to eat salad it is good for you."

"How come things are good for you taste terrible?" said one of the twin girls.

"That is how you *tell*," said Madelaine. "Eat salad, good for teeth and bones and eyes and stuff."

"Who says?" said the girl.

That little blister is going to be trouble, someone, all her damn life, Du Pre thought.

"Doctors say that," said Madelaine.

"They eat this stuff?" said the girl twin. "You ask them that, maybe. Maybe we get a pill don't have to chew so much."

"You," said Du Pré, "you got a name?"

"Marisa," said the little girl. She smiled. Even little white teeth.

"After dinner we call your Auntie Maria, you ask her that," said Du Pré. My youngest daughter, I think this is maybe her kid.

Take a pill, salad. I have heard this before.

"Auntie Maria call earlier," said Marisa.

I have heard this before, that damn kid, she is in goddamned England and still stirring the shit, back here, in Montana.

"She tell you to ask that?" said Du Pré.

"No," said Marisa.

Right, you little shit, you complain, the vegetables, Auntie Maria she say what she say about vegetables, tough being a kid. Got a good coach. Now I figure out where Maria get it, I am getting somewhere.

I never know shit about my women. I probably be safely dead before this little shit tear the country up too much. We got a damn rodeo queen here.

Old age it is a good thing you miss a lot.

"Grand-père," said Marisa, "Auntie Maria say her saddle is here somewhere."

Du Pré looked at her.

The little saddle that had been Du Pré's mother's.

"Yah, it is here," Du Pré said.

In a minute I remember where the fuck it is, I get no peace until I do.

"It is in the attic," said Madelaine. "In a big pink box says HAPPY BIRTHDAY on it."

Saved, Du Pré thought.

"Maria say I maybe use it," said Marisa.

Right, Du Pré thought, now all we got to do is find a horse go under the saddle.

"Eat your salad," said Du Pré.

Little Marisa grimly chewed up every shred of greens, never once taking her eyes off Du Pré's.

I give up now, Du Pré thought, another one tougher than me. They mostly are.

Okay, that damn Bart got horses he don't need. I go and see Booger Tom tomorrow.

"Grand-père," said Marisa, "I ask you a question?"

Du Pré stared at her.

Sure, you little flower, like, you need another saddle, horse, for your twin sister.

"My twin sister, Gertrude, she need a saddle, horse, too."

"Gertrude?"

"My name it is not Ger-trooood," said Marisa's sister. "It is Berne."

"How old you two?" asked Du Pré.

"Seven," said the twins.

"Don't make horses small enough for you, I get you a couple of goats."

The twins looked horrified.

"Your grand-père full of shit," said Madelaine. "He already got two horses picked out. Just got to get that saddle, have a new one made."

"Thank you, Grand-père," said Marisa and Berne.

Thank you, Madelaine, thought Du Pré, guess I go to the attic and then tomorrow I go, the saddlemaker.

Drive to Miles City.

Okay.

"You are excused," said Madelaine, "no dessert tonight."

Wails.

"Well, okay," said Madelaine. "Just wanted to know, you are asleep."

Giggles.

Plum dump cake.

Du Pré had two pieces.

The kids all filed out with their dishes and silverware and Du Pré heard the stuff being flung in the restaurant-sized dishwasher in the kitchen. The kitchen had expanded since the house was Du Pré's, out fifteen feet, and a big gas stove and double refrigerator added. A big chopping-block table in the middle of the room. Huge restaurant pots.

Got me a damn Army, I maybe start a war with someone.

"Ver' good you are," said Madelaine. "Now maybe you go, get that little saddle."

Du Pré didn't bother asking her how she knew where it was.

Thirteen kids, I need thirteen saddles and then another thirteen saddles and a stock ranch and a full-time harness maker and boot maker, too.

"Marisa and Berne want to do that fancy riding," said Madelaine, as she carried serving dishes into the kitchen.

"We give them all, Bart," said Du Pré, "He got the money and a good heart."

"Yah," said Madelaine, "well, Marisa and Berne they see this movie and they want, do that."

Du Pré didn't have to ask what movie.

"These horses they got to be *black*," he said.

"Good idea," said Madelaine.

Bart for sure.

Du Pré helped Madelaine stow the rest of the dishes in the dishwasher and then he went to the hallway and he reached up and pulled down the ladder. A little dust fell. It smelled like the house he grew up in.

Du Pré found a flashlight and he crawled up the ladder and into the attic. It was very warm. There was new insulation in the roof.

Boxes and trunks and more boxes.

One scarred leather trunk, old and broken-hinged.

Brought down from Canada, 1887, when we run from those English.

Pret' much everything us own in that, a wagon, a rifle, shovel and hoe, couple old horses.

English steal all the good horses.

Make a life here, pick them mussels, the river, sell the shells to button makers. Only cash money.

Buffalo are gone.

Cobwebs brushed Du Pré's face.

He saw the box. Pink with HAPPY BIRTHDAY in big green letters on the side.

Du Pré moved the cartons on top of it and then he tugged it back to the opening in the ceiling. He let it bump on the steps till he could step on the floor and lift and set it down.

Dust.

Madelaine came with a rag and she wiped it.

Du Pré carried it into the kitchen and set it on the counter in the center of the room. He opened the top, the flaps folded over each other to hold it shut.

Tissue paper and the smell of neat's-foot oil.

The tissue paper was yellow and crackled like fire when Du Pré pulled it out.

Little saddle, made by them Coggeshalls, Miles City.

Her father get it for her.

Mama, Papa, they are dead a long time. Still here, though.

Du Pré lifted the saddle out. Some of the leathers were bent wrong from sitting in the box. But there was still a little moisture on the seat, little tiny yellow beads of oil.

Maria only put this up, eight years ago maybe.

Seems a long time.

"That is a good thing," said Madelaine.

Du Pré nodded.

Give Marisa and Berne saddles, horses.

Give them their people.

♣ CHAPTER 7 ♣

I just told him I didn't want any part of it," said Bart. "He was quite rude."

Du Pré laughed.

Messmer wanted a lake. He had the water but not the hole.

Bart got a billion dollars maybe, digs basements, irrigation ditches, stock ponds. Keeps him less crazy. I got my fiddle, weighs maybe six or eight ounces, he got a dragline weighs thirty tons.

"I didn't like him," said Bart.

Du Pré nodded.

Susan Klein was watching an author babble about a book the interviewer for the television program hadn't read.

Um, George, what is your book about? How did you get your ideas for the book? The author looked pissed. The author was also thinking about how many more copies of his book would sell because this fucking idiot who hadn't read his book was asking him questions in front of millions of TV watchers.

Du Pré thought of musicologists who had asked the same dumb question about Métis' music. My fiddling. What is it about? Where, me, I get my ideas?

Don't know. I just do it.

We been doin' it couple thousand years maybe. Longer. Métis' music, people's music, how long people making music? Since maybe we sing our way through the wilderness, across the ice, the sea.

"He's a bad 'un," said Bart.

Messmer had shipped all the cattle, the ones he didn't have the hands shoot. He'd sold them dirt cheap. Some ranch out near the Dakotas.

Take them cows he shoot off his taxes, you bet.

Guy got to be a Republican, they do things that way.

"You going to play Sunday?" said Bart.

Du Pré nodded.

"Saturday night, Sunday afternoon," he said. Bassman and Père Godin coming through. Wonder what no-deposit burlap-blonde Bassman have with him this time. Guy goes through them like soap.

"Wonder what flavor of blonde Bassman'll have this time?" said Bart.

"We sell tickets," said Du Pré, "make some money."

Bassman smoked so much marijuana he smelled like a field of hemp on fire. Never missed a beat.

Père Godin, the old fart, had seventy-one acknowledged illegitimate children.

"He really like women," Madelaine had explained. "Women, they can tell that, want to have his babies. He like babies, too."

Du Pré sipped his whiskey and he rolled a smoke.

The telephone rang and Susan Klein answered it. She said something and she nodded to Du Pré.

Madelaine want me home, watch the monsters at the table, Du Pré thought.

Susan handed the phone over the bar.

"Gabriel," said Harvey Wallace, aka Harvey Weasel Fat, Blackfeet and FBI.

Du Pré grunted.

"Now, Gabriel," said Harvey, "you ain't heard my pitch yet."

"I am old, tired, want to drink, sleep, play a little music," said

Du Pré. "You call, I get no sleep, drink too much, don't play music, maybe get shot at, something. Maybe I hang up, you call back I am gone, no one knows where."

Du Pré liked Harvey well enough but Harvey liked the law and so if things fell wrong Du Pré would spend his life in prison. Harvey was quite clear about that. It was a big thing between them.

"I got something I thought I'd ask you to look after for me," said Harvey.

"Yeah," said Du Pré. "That asshole Messmer, you love him, are jealous, want to know his every move."

"I *like* him," said Harvey. "When I *love* somebody I arrest their ass, put them away for fucking *ever*."

"Yeah," said Du Pré.

Little monsters, feeding time, pillow fight, story, what do I need this for?

"There's a dead woman down in Wyoming," said Harvey.

"No woman ever die, Wyoming before," said Du Pré. "It is some news you give me, Harvey."

"This one was shot in the head and burned in her car," said Harvey.

"Watch too much TV," said Du Pré, "down in that Wyoming. Violence, you know."

"She was burned up pretty good," said Harvey. "Car was gutted. But then there was the meat in the trunk."

Du Pré sighed.

"There was a big cooler of frozen meat in the trunk," said Harvey, "which did not come through the fire all that well, but there was this receipt stuck to a package of filet mignon which was interesting."

Fuck. Thought Du Pré.

"Fancy steaks, this Messmer asshole," said Du Pré.

"Not quite," said Harvey, "but it reminded me of Messmer."

Du Pré waited.

"Some of the meat wasn't meat," said Harvey.

Du Pré sighed.

"Some of the meat was heroin," said Harvey, "some was co-caine. Now, mind you, not whole packages or anything, but the paper the meat was wrapped in had traces of those drugs on it."

Du Pré sighed.

"You wake up, middle of the night," he said, "in that Washington, D.C., and you smell a car burning in Wyoming and say, honey, to your wife there, it is that Messmer burning up women in cars again, him I smell."

Harvey sighed.

"We've been interested in Messmer for a while," he said.

Right, thought Du Pré, now this Messmer is out in Montana, Harvey don't want to send a bunch of Mormons, those wingtip shoes, try to blend in with the sagebrush.

Need a damn 'breed like me.

"Anyway," said Harvey, "maybe you'd keep an eye on Messmer."

"No," said Du Pré.

"Madelaine there?" said Harvey.

"No," said Du Pré.

Tell my Madelaine Messmer is a child molester, then I am cooked, you Blackfeet son of a bitch.

"Well," said Harvey Weasel Fat, "when I get hold of Madelaine I will tell her that Messmer is a child molester."

Du Pré called Harvey a few names, the best ones were in Cree, about syphilis and skunks and sodomy and Harvey's mother.

"I am glad I don't speak Cree," said Harvey.

That is bullshit, too, Du Pré thought.

"Okay," said Du Pré, "my good friend Harvey Weasel Fat, what you want to fuck out of me, eh?"

"Can always count on you, Gabriel," said Harvey, "but you don't go scalping anybody."

Métis don't scalp, but Harvey know that, too.

"Messmer is what the old biker gangs have turned into," said Harvey. "They deal in drugs, weapons, women, stolen autos, extortion, arson, and murder. Usual bad-guy stuff. Messmer is up in it to his pink and shell-like ears. He's smart as hell, many arrests, no convictions. Witnesses die or suffer memory loss. Alibis hold. Now we understand he's cleaned the ranch out. Going to raise horses. My ass. I would like to know what goes on there."

Du Pré sipped his whiskey.

"Gabriel?" said Harvey. "This guy is a danger to your community."

"So are you FBI bastards," said Du Pré.

"Yeah," said Harvey, "but our manners are better. We fuck up, we apologize."

Du Pré snorted.

"How much you want to know?" said Du Pré.

"Bad," said Harvey, "bad as I ever wanted to know anything."

"Okay," said Du Pré.

"Madelaine home," said Harvey, "her place?" In perfect Cree.

"No," said Du Pré.

"Well," said Harvey, "I'll just hang up and try a couple numbers."

"Prick," said Du Pré.

"Okay," said Harvey, "Call me tomorrow, I am too busy to call Madelaine tonight."

"Asshole," said Du Pré.

"Everybody's got one," said Harvey. He hung up.

Du Pré shut the phone down but he didn't put it back in its cradle.

He looked at Bart.

Bart looked at him.

"Harvey?" said Bart.

Du Pré nodded.

"I guess," said Bart, "we have us a lake to dig."

❧ CHAPTER 8 ❧

Du Pré drove to Miles City in the rain. It was a heavy rain, the water lifted up from the Indian Ocean weeks before and pushed across the Pacific and hooked through British Columbia and shoved down to Montana and dumped. It rained very little on the High Plains, except for storms like these, which made boiling rivers in dry canyons.

It rained so hard Du Pré drove sixty.

It took a long time to get to Miles City.

Once Du Pré had to stop, and watch a wall of water eight feet high rip out a fence. And then it was gone and only the marks of its tread in the grass remained, and the corpse of a fox stuck in the barbed wire. The fence was down flat on the road.

Du Pré got out and cut the wire in several places. The whole fence was clotted with sticks and grass. He pulled heavy sections off to the verge. A cattle hauler headed the other way pulled up just as Du Pré dropped the last of the mess out of the way. The driver honked and put on some speed.

Du Pré crossed the Yellowstone River just before he got to the town. It was still clear. In a few hours it wouldn't be.

He parked in front of the saddler's and got out in the pelting rain; he fished the little saddle out of the trunk and went on in. The old man he had dealt with before was sitting on a chair in front of the cash register. Two younger men were working on leather in the back.

"You," said the old man. He got up and went to the back; he came back with two small saddles, plain, bright yellow-brown leather, and a pair of bridles of the same leather, with simple bits and brass buckles.

Du Pré laughed.

"I come to ask you to make those," he said.

"Your wife called a year ago," said the old man. "We got a hell of a backlog."

"What I owe you?" asked Du Pré.

"Paid," said the old man.

Du Pré bought some gloves and a couple of little heavy saddle blankets; he looked at the black velvet shelf in the glass case that held the cash register and he saw a silver and turquoise ring, a big old one with the ragged, uneven marks of handwork with simple tools. The stone was a fair one, deep in color and veined a little in black.

Du Pré bought that, too, for a hundred dollars. It fit his middle finger on his left hand.

He put the three saddles in the car and got in and went to a gas station; he filled both tanks, the one the car had come with and the other that sat up in the trunk.

The rain was fairing off and by the time he went back across the bridge the Yellowstone had come up four feet and it was dirty and filled with trees and trash.

In an hour the roads were dry enough so he could cruise at a hundred and ten. There would sometimes be pools of water at the bottom of hills where culverts had been plugged with debris, but none so deep he had to fish out the crap before he could go on.

He was back in Toussaint by ten o'clock at night.

Du Pré stopped at the saloon and went in. Susan Klein was watching a program about Picasso on television. She was nodding her head and only filling orders during commercials.

She got Du Pré a whiskey ditch during an expensive, elegant advertisement for bad bulk wine which would get the drinker laid in lovely seaside surroundings, to the music of Louis Armstrong, sort of.

"Got the saddles?" said Susan Klein.

Du Pré nodded. One woman here know something they all know it.

Susan Klein filled several orders and made change and went back to her stool to listen to some white-haired fool explain Picasso some more.

Du Pré reached over the bar and got the telephone, then he called Madelaine.

"Ha," said Madelaine, "I play a little joke on you."

"He maybe mail the saddles," said Du Pré, "it is a long drive."

"Du Pré," said Madelaine, "you maybe think on the drive, yes?"

Shit.

"That Harvey is dangerous," said Madelaine. "He want you do things he can't. This Messmer is a bad guy. Smart."

Du Pré hadn't thought of much at all. The rain. It was not a good thinking day. Gray and peaceful and close about, couldn't see much.

"Okay," said Du Pré.

"So you don't think about this at all?" said Madelaine.

"No," said Du Pré.

"Harvey is not your friend, Du Pré," said Madelaine. "He wants to put you in jail."

He got plenty reasons, that.

"So I maybe think down here a while," said Du Pré.

"Yah," said Madelaine, "you think a while half hour and I need some pink wine maybe, bag of barbecue chips."

"Okay," said Du Pré.

He put the telephone back.

She is afraid. She is not afraid I go after them guys killing the women, not afraid before. She is a warrior lady but she is afraid. She don't do the ululation this time, don't do the throat sing for her man.

Don't make sense.

Susan Klein came to Du Pré when the white-haired fool explaining Picasso stopped in favor of a car ad for some car to roar across the Nevada salt flats in.

Susan Klein put a paper sack on the counter. Pink wine and chips and a bottle of bourbon.

"You need tobacco?" said Susan.

She had thousands of sacks of Bull Durham the previous owner had bought from a salesman for reasons Du Pré thought about but really didn't want to know.

Du Pré nodded.

The door opened and Booger Tom walked in. The old cowboy was half drunk and his red face was split in a wide grin.

"Oh, joy," said Susan. "See if that old bastard has a gun, will you? I don't need any more damn holes in the roof."

Booger Tom spotted Du Pré and stumped over in his worn custom boots. They had once been elegant, but now they had bands of duct tape around the ball of the foot.

"DOO-PRÉ!" said Booger Tom. His breath was so foul Du Pré reeled back.

The old cowboy didn't get drunk very often but when he did he made a job of it. Du Pré looked at him.

"You don't got no gun?" he said.

Booger Tom looked puzzled.

"What the hell you want with my damn gun?" he said. He pulled it out, a big old Peacemaker with worn ivory grips, the gun of choice for train robbers.

Du Pré sighed.

"Give me the damn gun or I don't let you drink," said Du Pré.

Booger Tom considered that for a long moment. Then he handed over the gun.

Du Pré tucked it under the counter on the far side.

Booger Tom attempted to mount the barstool and ride the sucker.

He kept slipping off.

"Where's the damn stirrups?" the old man muttered.

"Tom," said Susan Klein, "you better go on home now. I won't serve you."

Booger Tom paused in his attempt to ride the wild bar stool.

"Sure is drunk out tonight, missy," he said.

Susan Klein smiled softly at him.

"Tom," she said, "Gabriel will take you home."

"I think," said Booger Tom, "that is a ver' good 'dea."

Du Pré picked up the paper sack.

He nodded to Susan and led the old cowboy out of the bar and down the steps to his cruiser.

He opened the passenger door and helped the drunk old man in. He shut the door.

Du Pré walked around behind the car and set the bag in and then he slid in.

"April Fool," said Booger Tom. He was his feral and alert self again.

Du Pré looked at him.

"What is this?" said Du Pré.

"Benetsee wants you to come," said Pelon, Benetsee's apprentice. He had been sitting quietly in the back seat.

"Okay," said Du Pré.

He started the car and drove away.

✤ CHAPTER 9 ✤

Benetsee slept at his table, his head on his arm. He snored loudly. His mouth was open and the stubs of his brown old teeth had silver bubbles on them.

Du Pré poured a jar of cheap fizzy wine. He set it in front of the old man. He rolled a thick cigarette and set it by the jar of yellow screwtop.

Benetsee slept on.

"He do this," said Pelon, "he sleep, two days, there."

Benetsee farted magnificently.

"I never heard him in such good voice," said Booger Tom. "Pretty words, too."

Benetsee's eyes opened.

"Ver' few brains, this room," he said.

"Fewer since your old ass woke up," said Booger Tom. "Now you mind maybe explainin' why I got dragged out here, listen to some old fart fart?"

Benetsee sat up. He looked at Booger Tom and Du Pré. Pelon had drifted off. Du Pré hadn't even heard him go.

"I am lonely," said Benetsee, "hard to play that pigknuckle alone."

He put his old brown hand, a claw like a bird's, around the jar and he lifted it and drank it down, a good pint of bad wine. He belched. He put the cigarette in his mouth and Booger Tom lit it with a cheap butane lighter. The flame was set high and it licked Benetsee's eyebrows.

The old man ignored that, and he drew a deep draw on the smoke.

"I got to go, north," he said. "Pelon, too. You will be all right."

Du Pré sighed.

He means something ver' bad happen, thought Du Pré, and I need him and he is off being a goddamned raven or something.

"Your papa," said Benetsee, "bury pretty stones, a metal box, but you know who find them for you."

Du Pré nodded.

My papa, Catfoot, he kill Bart's brother, hide a necklace and money, brass box in the lilac roots. Somebody hang a chunk of meat out of reach, birds peck the suet, pieces fall.

Coyote he scratch at the snow, little frozen chunks of fat. I dig there. Truth is a sad thing sometimes.

Benetsee looked up at Du Pré.

He held out his glass jar and Du Pré filled it and the old man drank off the wine.

He stood up and he pulled up his pants and then he walked out the door.

Du Pré waited as long as a piss took.

"He is gone, Pelon," said Du Pré.

Booger Tom nodded.

Du Pré blew out the flame in the kerosene lantern and turned the wick down so the fuel wouldn't evaporate so fast.

They went out and Du Pré pulled the door shut and put the hook in the eye. The old man never locked the cabin, and once years ago a couple of bad kids had come in to find what they could steal.

It was night.

They were found the next morning miles away, cut and bruised from running into things.

When the Sheriff tried to start the old car they were driving to move it to town and look it over, since a number of other houses out in the country had been robbed by these kids, the car wouldn't start. He lifted up the hood and bare wires gleamed and porcupine droppings sat on the engine.

The kids were so terrified they couldn't even speak about what had frightened them, something about birds and dogs.

The Sheriff found some loot in the trunk of the car and the boys went off to the state school.

When the tow truck driver went out to get the car, he tried the key and the engine caught just like that.

Du Pré had a snort of whiskey from the plastic bottle he kept under the seat of the old cruiser and offered the bottle to Booger Tom. The old man shook his head.

"Too tired," he said.

Du Pré wallowed the old cruiser down to the county road over rocks and ruts and turned off toward Bart's.

"So you want some advice," said Booger Tom, "ask a coyote. That old bastard is one fine joker."

"Yeah," said Du Pré.

"When I first come West," said Booger Tom, "I was fresh meat to some of them old boys. We's ridin' up in the mountains and come on a grizzly and ever'body set off to rope the damn bear. I went along. I could rope pretty good, practiced since I was a pup, and my ridin' was fine, and I busted out a little ahead and got my loop on the bear. My advice, don't do that. The bear grabbed the rope in his jaws and jerked me and my horse over and then lit out after me. I was so damn eager to prove myself they let me. Not one of them old bastards had tossed a loop but they sure got me to."

Du Pré laughed.

"The bear ate me of course," said Booger Tom. "I am not really here."

They crested a hill and saw Bart's big mercury lamps flaring a few miles away. They dropped down and the lights sank behind the next hill.

A mule deer buck froze in the headlights, the tapetum flaring glassy neon red. Du Pré slowed and the dazzled deer ran back and forth for a moment and then it jumped the barbed wire fence and was gone.

"That squirrelly son of a bitch is just lookin' for a windshield to come through," said Booger Tom.

"Yeah," said Du Pré. He'd had two do that very thing. He'd had to dive for the floor while the deer took his seat. Both times Du Pré had switched off the ignition, and both times the car he was driving ended up rolling and Du Pré crawled out when the car stopped, covered with deer blood and glass.

Bart was out doing something to the hydraulic lines on the backhoe. He had socket sets and some valves and new hose spread on a blue plastic sheet on a folding worktable.

Du Pré drove Booger Tom to the door of his cabin and let the old man get out and go on in. He was tired and old.

He drove back to where Bart was working.

Man worth maybe hundreds of millions would have been happier poor.

"We do that tomorrow?" said Bart.

"Pret' wet," said Du Pré.

"Day after, then," said Bart. "Turns my stomach to work for that bastard. But I can always quit."

"Harvey know him," said Du Pré.

"Yes," said Bart, "not an admirable life the man has lived."

"They are not here, raising horses," said Du Pré.

"No shit," said Bart.

Du Pré handed Bart a socket and Bart snapped off the one he had on the ratchet and put the new one on and he handed the other socket to Du Pré, who put it in the case.

"That teacher Porterfield say this one is like the old man started that ranch," said Du Pré.

"I suspect they were all like him, the old ones," said Bart. "Every fortune is founded on a crime."

Du Pré laughed. Bart's family money stank of blood. Bootlegging, theft, extortion, illegal gambling, prostitution, murder, corruption, and how can you sin by coveting when you take whatever you see? So Bart said of his family.

"Harvey wants to know what they do," said Du Pré.

"So why doesn't Harvey send some of his agents?" said Bart.

"He don't think Mormons in wingtips blend in so good," said Du Pré.

"Yeah," said Bart, "I see."

"How big is this lake?" said Du Pré.

"It'll be a good half-mile across when it fills," said Bart. "Great little dam site if you like dams."

Du Pré grunted. The Fort Peck and Garrison dams on the Missouri had ruined many people, ranchers, farmers, Indians.

The Missouri Breaks were underwater mostly.

Catfoot's favorite country.

"I got bad feeling this," said Du Pré.

Bart nodded and tightened a fitting with a pair of channel locks.

"We've had worse, I expect," said Bart.

It is not the wild horse that throws you, Du Pré thought, it is the one that you think is broke to riding.

"What to do, what to do," said Bart. "I guess I will do a little earth-moving and general-purpose environmental destruction."

Coyotes started to sing in the foothills. Rabbit-running song that ended when the rabbit's life did.

Du Pré was tired. He yawned.

He drove to his old house, full of his grandchildren.

♣ CHAPTER 10 ♣

Larry Messmer stood on a small knoll in his irrigation boots and three-piece suit, his eyes behind dark glasses and his hands in his pants pockets. The wind tugged at his coat and hair. He did not move.

Bart dropped the giant dragline's bucket and he dragged it and it filled with earth, the splintered bones of the Wolf Mountains carried down by water.

Du Pré jammed the front-end loader into the pile of yellow-brown earth and lifted the bucket and turned the loader around and dumped the earth into the big dump truck. He glanced at the huge leaf springs.

One more load and it is full.

After the next load Du Pré put the loader in neutral and locked the brakes and he got down and then up into the big truck and drove down to where the dam was rising. The soil was not good for building dams. When the dam was done they would face the inside with bentonite. The fine white clay would take on water and swell and seal the earth.

Deep Creek carried a fair amount of water, but still not enough to wash the dumped earth away. Bart had scraped earth into a small coulee with his huge bulldozer and blocked it and the creek was filling the depression behind. It would take another winter to fill, and by then a concrete spillway would be laid down the face, to carry the excess water.

The creek bed below still ran water, a few inches that came up through a bed of gravel. The water behind the dam was filthy, thick with mud, the water below clear.

Streams here run under the earth, Du Pré remembered Catfoot saying.

Catfoot had looked for old streams to dig for gold in.

Bart shut off Popsicle, his huge dragline, and he rumbled over to the tiny dam in his huge bulldozer and bladed more earth into the little coulee.

Bart shut the dozer off and Du Pré rolled up the window of the dump truck, then shut off the front-end loader and backhoe and tipped up the seat.

Messmer was still standing on the knoll. He hadn't moved.

Bart and Du Pré got in Du Pré's old cruiser and drove off.

Du Pré looked in his rearview mirror.

Messmer was still standing there.

When they got to the Toussaint Bar, Susan Klein looked up from some beadwork and smiled happily.

"Customers!" she said, "I am at a critical juncture, so get your own damn drinks and if you want food go cook it."

She bent her head back to her work.

A couple old men sat at a table with red beers half gone in front of them.

There were no other customers, it was April and very busy on the ranches.

Du Pré went behind the bar and he filled a tall glass with ice for Bart and grabbed the soda gun and filled the glass. He slid it over and then he made a tall whiskey ditch for himself and pulled a bag of potato chips from the rack and put them by his drink, then he came back around and sat next to Bart.

"How's the destruction of the environment going?" asked

Susan Klein. "Benny half expects he'll end up arresting you two for felonious water molesting or something."

"Messmer has a permit," said Bart.

"No doubt," said Susan Klein.

The door opened and two men and a woman came in. They all took off their dark glasses and they blinked at the dim light rising. The woman pointed to a table and they sat, looking over at the bar.

Susan Klein tied a knot and she put down her beadwork and walked over.

"Afternoon," she said. "Want anything?"

Two bottles of imported beer and a glass of sherry.

The woman took off her jacket. She had on a thick dark red sweater and a heavy gold chain, flat links like a snake's body.

Susan Klein took the drinks over.

"Could you tell us how to get to the Messmer ranch?" said the woman.

Susan Klein told her.

"Damn ass end of nowhere," said one of the men.

"Yeah," said Susan Klein, "but we like it."

Du Pré looked over.

The man who hadn't spoken drank a little beer. He was big and his neck was thick. He had tight gold ringlets, like a shower cap. His eyes were puffy.

Du Pré glanced up at the stuffed gray owl that sat on a shelf to the left of the big old scabby mirror that took up twelve feet of the bar back.

The owl's left eye was a camera lens. Bart had gotten the camera for Susan Klein when some saloons up north had been robbed.

Maybe she turn the damn thing on, Du Pré thought, maybe not.

The three finished their drinks and they left.

Susan Klein went over. She hooted.

They had left a fifty-dollar bill on the table.

Susan waved it.

"If they just don't come back," she said, "I'll think more kindly of them. Gave me the damn creeps."

Du Pré laughed.

"You got the camera maybe going?" he said.

Susan nodded.

"It comes on when the door opens," she said, "and if there's any movement in the bar it stays on."

Du Pré nodded.

Susan went back in the kitchen and in a few minutes she came back with the cassette. She handed it to Du Pré.

"Let me guess," she said, "Harvey Weasel Fat Wallace would like to look at this."

Du Pré nodded.

"Cop's wife," said Bart.

"Benny is a sheriff in a county that has fewer people in it than most big city blocks do," said Susan Klein, "and he does his job as well as he can. Which is mostly listening, and Benny likes to listen. He breaks up fights between man and wife well. But this shit is not his meat. No, A Little Voice Called Me."

Susan grinned.

"If you give me that I'll send it to Harvey," said Bart.

Bart had a lot of expensive electronic gear in his house Du Pré did not like and did not care to know very much about.

"Time's a-wasting," said Susan Klein.

"You didn't like them?" said Bart.

"They gave me the fucking willies," said Susan Klein. Her cussing was a sore point with Benny, who used no word stronger than *gosh*.

Bart nodded. He pulled his little folding telephone out of his jacket pocket and he pressed a button that dialed a number automatically. He waited. For several minutes.

"Hello," said Bart, ". . . you are allowed to do that. Uh, I think we may have a problem . . . very bad people. I don't know that . . ."

Bart said yes and he said no for a while.

He said good-bye.

He picked up the cassette.

Du Pré got up and he and Bart went out to Du Pré's old cruiser and headed off to Bart's ranch.

Du Pré dropped him off and he waved to Booger Tom who was working a young horse in a round corral. The old man touched his hat brim but never took his eyes off the horse.

Du Pré stopped for a badger that was standing in the road. The animal sniffed and sniffed. It finally decided it did not want to eat Du Pré's old cruiser and it went off the road and down into the barrow pit. Du Pré smiled and went on.

He thought of the badger he had raised from a baby. The badger fed from his hand and followed Du Pré around and then one day the badger hissed and bit Du Pré on the soft flesh of his left hand and it ran into the brush. It came back when it was hungry but Du Pré would not feed it anymore.

"Needs to be wild," said Catfoot. "Now maybe you know about that."

Du Pré still had little stippled white scars on his hand, marks of the badger's teeth.

He turned into the drive that led up to his old house where Madelaine and his grandchildren were.

Doors and windows are still on, that is a good sign.

Du Pré went up the steps and into the house, which was full of good food smells.

It was quiet.

Five kids sat in the living room looking sad.

" 'Nother ten minutes," said Madelaine from the kitchen, "they can't talk."

Du Pré shrugged. They'd done something but he did not really care what that was.

♣ CHAPTER 11 ♣

T his a pret' fancy truck," said Raymond. He was lying on a heavy chaise longue, the back tipped up, like a hospital bed. He had a lot of plaster on him and a few stitches but no IV lines.

Bart's huge Chevy Suburban had seats that were removable. Jacqueline sat beside her husband, on a folding chair, the kind that packers use for really expensive dudes.

Du Pré kept the heavy vehicle at eighty. He didn't want to tip it over.

My cruiser is better. Eighty. Bah.

There was a small cooler on the passenger seat. Du Pré flipped up the lid and he grabbed a bag of peppered beef slices and he chewed some.

Jacqueline leaned around the seat and she pulled out two beers and she popped the tabs. Raymond took one.

"Me, I have to pee again soon," he said.

The hospital had sent along a plastic jug of peculiar shape for just that moment.

Jacqueline handed him the jug.

"Don't look at me," said Raymond.

"Papa," said Jacqueline, "this fool think I never see his damn dick before. Me, I know it better than him, see it closer than he ever will."

Du Pré grunted. He lifted the bottle of whiskey he had stuck down beside the seat and drank some, then he capped it and put

60

it back. He fished out his old tobacco pouch and he rolled a smoke and lit it.

"Rear window," said Jacqueline.

Du Pré felt for the button and pressed it and the window slid down and Jacqueline emptied the jug.

Du Pré pressed the button and the window came back up.

A light bar began to flash.

"Oh, Papa," said Jacqueline, "I see his wipers go on."

Shit. I am in my cruiser I turn on mine they leave me alone.

A siren wailed.

Du Pré pulled over on the edge of the pavement and he slowed and then he stopped.

Du Pré dropped a jacket over the whiskey bottle.

He looked in the rearview mirror. The Highway Patrol car sat there with the light bar flashing.

The patrolwoman got out. She was small and blonde and she held herself very erect. She wore wraparound mirrored sunglasses and all of the cop stuff, including a big stainless-steel automatic.

Du Pré rolled down his window.

"Could I see your driver's license and registration, sir?" she said.

"Don't got either one," said Du Pré. "Me, I got this, though." He opened his wallet and showed her his brand inspector's badge.

"Very nice," said the patrolwoman. "Could you get out of the car, sir?"

Du Pré flicked his cigarette off on the highway and he opened the door and got out.

"You smell strongly of alcohol," said the patrolwoman, "and you do not have either a license or a registration for this vehicle?"

Du Pré shook his head.

Jacqueline had gotten out of the far side of the Suburban.

"Ma'am!" barked the patrolwoman, "please stay in the car!"

Jacqueline walked around the front of the vehicle.

"Bullshit. I stay in the damn car," she said. "My husband he is all banged up and my Papa he is driving us home and why you are stopping us?"

"Ma'am," said the patrolwoman, "I must ask you to get back in the vehicle."

"No," said Jacqueline.

The patrolwoman backed away toward her car, hand near her gun, and she reached in and grabbed her radio mike and she spoke rapidly.

"Ver' good," said Du Pré, "pret' soon we have two dozen Highway cops here, helicopters, riot squad."

"Oh, Papa," said Jacqueline, "this is crap."

She walked back toward the patrolwoman, who told her to stop.

These daughters, mine, Du Pré thought, pains in the ass. I maybe get out of jail, next Christmas.

He tried to remember the last time he had renewed his driver's license. He couldn't. He took out his wallet and he found it and he checked the expiration date.

1981.

Du Pré opened the door and reached over to the glove box and opened it. The registration was in a plastic holder along with the cards proving that the insurance was current.

Du Pré got back out and stood there.

Jacqueline was talking to the patrolwoman from fifteen feet away.

"You trying to kill my poor husband?" she said.

Du Pré chewed some licorice.

Should have brought my damn cruiser.

Damn daughter maybe not throw a bucket of piss on a Highway Patrol car that would help, too.

A siren in the distance, coming from the north.

That guy maybe know me, Du Pré thought, I hope.

Damn laws anyway.

Jacqueline and the patrolwoman were faced off glaring at each other.

The siren got closer.

The lights of a Highway Patrol car came over the hill.

Du Pré rolled a smoke and lit it.

The patrol car slowed down and pulled off on the far side of the road. The patrolman got out.

Ah, that McPhie, thought Du Pré, I know him some.

McPhie was a huge man, red-faced and gray-haired. He had gone a little to fat but not much. He had once played pro football for a short time. He had come to hear Du Pré play a few times, bringing his wife.

"Ma'am," said McPhie, looking at Jacqueline, "could you go and join your father, there?"

McPhie stood so Du Pré could not see the small blonde patrolwoman behind his bulk.

He was talking to her. She was yelling at him.

Finally she got in her car and shut off the light bar and she started the engine and turned around and roared away.

McPhie stood still, watching her go. He turned around and he ambled back to Du Pré.

"Afternoon, Jacqueline," said McPhie. "Would you please leave me and your dad alone a moment?"

Jacqueline looked at Du Pré. He nodded. She got back in the Suburban.

"Thanks," said Du Pré.

McPhie nodded.

"Mr. Du Pré," he said, "we sort of know each other and I know a bit about you, and you are a good man. But we need to get a few things straight, here. First, it is damn near the next century and the frontier has been dead, I am told, for about a hundred years . . ."

Du Pré nodded.

"Used to was, feller could handle his liquor, and didn't ram a damn school bus, no one much cared they drank and drove or not. But then, Mr. Du Pré, about thirty fucking years ago all that changed. Now, I am not all that thrilled to be busting people for bad breath, but the law allows it now, and they fucking well mean business."

Du Pré nodded.

"Officer Parker there is a good officer and had your daughter not been mouthy your sorry ass would be right in Officer Parker's patrol car, headed for the nearest place gives Breathalyzer tests, which you would fucking well flunk. She then would put you in jail. You would then go to court and lose the license—let me see that damn thing . . ."

Du Pré handed McPhie his driver's license.

"I've seen older ones out here in the sagebrush," said McPhie, "but that's pretty good. Pretty damn good."

McPhie looked off into the distance.

"I enjoy the hell out of your music," he said. He smiled, his big red face all jolly. He rocked on his boot heels.

"However, I must inform you that things are different here in good old Montana than they were the last fucking time you checked decades ago. We are an actual state right in the Union, the United States of America, with a Legislature filled with pissants as dumb and awful as any larger and better known state. They pass laws, to while away the time, and you, Du Pré, have broken about five of 'em."

Du Pré waited.

"I know that here in the sagebrush it is easy to forget that these pissants in Helena are there passing their laws, but it is so. They pay fools like me to enforce 'em, and I do, best I can."

McPhie placed one of his giant, meaty hands on Du Pré's shoulder.

"If I catch you pulling this bullshit, your ass goes to jail, you lose the license you are going to get tomorrow, and you can work out the rest with the judge. I cleaned up after you this one time, on account of your reputation and essentially primitive nature. If you get nailed by Officer Parker, she makes up for being blonde and cute by being as mean as a snake. You get nailed by me I will make her look downright benevolent."

McPhie looked at Du Pré.

"You hear anything I said?" he said.

"Sure," said Du Pré. "Thanks for likin' my music."

McPhie shrugged and nodded and he went off to his cruiser.

✤ CHAPTER 12 ✤

"This is pret' good, eh, Du Pré?" said Madelaine. They were lying in bed at her house.

Very quiet.

"They are good kids them," said Madelaine, "but I been there some, so have you, Du Pré."

Du Pré grunted. He didn't know exactly where the conversation was going so it wasn't time to agree yet.

"Jacqueline she say you get stopped by the cops. She throw pee on one of them, she is not looking."

Du Pré grunted.

"That big cop McPhie he chew your ass out," said Madelaine.

Du Pré grunted.

"Someday you get stopped and arrested, Du Pré," said Madelaine. "I know you, you will not like that."

Du Pré grunted.

Madelaine sighed. She got up and went off and then Du Pré heard the shower running.

He rolled a smoke and lit it and he dressed, leaving the cigarette in the ashtray while he pulled on his boots.

He went to the kitchen and made himself a drink. It was dark out but not very late.

I am glad, me, I don't got to watch all them kids feed like a bunch of starving coyotes. Ah, it is too quiet here. They take good damn care that Raymond.

Madelaine came back, combing her long black hair, all shot with silver. Red lights still played in it, and in her eyes.

"Ah," she said, "we go to that Toussaint Saloon, we have some pink wine, we don't got to ride herd on all them kids."

They drove the half-mile to the saloon.

Susan Klein was behind the bar and the place was pretty full, thirty or so people at the bar and the tables. A couple of cowboys were playing pool.

"Free at last," said Susan Klein, when they got to the bar.

She pushed their drinks over.

"Hear ol' McPhie chewed your ass," she said.

Du Pré grunted.

"Okay," said Susan Klein, "I can see it is a sore subject. God-damn interferin' government, tramplin' on the rights of good citizens who are just driving at a hundred and twenty with a bot-tle of rotgut in them. On the dirt roads . . ."

Du Pré grunted.

He had a good long swallow of his drink.

Susan Klein filled him up.

She went off whistling to check the tables.

All my friends they are layin' for me, Du Pré thought, news it travels ver' fast here. Next son of a bitch who asks me how my ass is, McPhie's teeth marks in it, I maybe hit them.

Bart came in. He saw Madelaine and Du Pré and he came up and sat by Du Pré.

"Heard McPhie almost arrested you for drunk driving," said Bart.

"Ah," said Madelaine, "you are lucky, Bart."

Bart looked around her.

"Du Pré was going to hit the next son of a bitch that asked about him, ass chewing, McPhie," said Madelaine, "but he like you too much."

"Oh no," said Bart. He was looking off at the door.

Harvey Wallace aka Weasel Fat Who Was Blackfeet and FBI was headed toward Du Pré and Madelaine.

"Harvey," said Madelaine, "you be quiet."

Du Pré looked at him.

"Balls," said Harvey. "I hear he almost got busted for drunk driving."

Du Pré dropped off the stool and threw a punch and Bart grabbed him while Harvey danced away.

"Touchy touchy," said Harvey. He was grinning hugely.

Du Pré stood stock-still, smiling.

"You are here," he said.

Harvey looked at the floor. He nodded. He shrugged.

"It seemed the place to be," he said.

"Them?" said Du Pré.

"Yeah," said Harvey, "very bad people. She's worse'n they are. Matter of fact, we had our local guys raid it soon as they could but there was no one there but that damn Messmer and the hands. Warrants out on all of them, but they are long gone."

Du Pré nodded. He got back on his bar stool.

"But I thought I would come anyway," said Harvey. "I like it here so much."

Oh, yes, Du Pré thought, Blackfeet who hates the outdoors. Loves oysters, jazz. Asphalt stinking in the sun. Yeah, you come here, you love the place so damn much.

"We need to talk," said Harvey, nodding toward the kitchen. There was a table in a little alcove there.

Du Pré followed him back.

Harvey got a cup of coffee when he passed the machine.

Du Pré sat down on the flat, hard bench. Harvey slid in across from him.

"Those people," said Harvey, "are wanted for murder. Several of them, matter of fact. The big guy, the one with the lamb's wool head, blew away six guys Messmer doesn't like, and the damn woman got two. Her name's Shannon Smiley. The ox is Clarence Gottmund. Willie Beeton is the other. Mean bunch. Sliced and diced a couple informants. They like to torture people."

Du Pré rolled a smoke.

"Messmer's parents' accident wasn't an accident," said Harvey.

Du Pré lit his cigarette.

"The bastard probably killed his sister back in '82," said Harvey.

Du Pré smoked.

Harvey drank coffee. He looked at Du Pré.

"These people," he said, "play very rough."

Du Pré nodded.

"I got to go there tomorrow," he said, "look at some horses. Raymond he is laid up a while."

Harvey pulled a sheaf of photographs from his pocket. He began to lay them out like playing cards. There were thirty-two of them.

Du Pré looked at the faces. They were all mug shots, all of men, hard-eyed, defiant, contemptuous. They looked like crooks. They were all white.

"Take long looks," said Harvey. "You see any of these charmers, I want to know."

Du Pré nodded.

"We want these people," said Harvey.

"They all come here?" said Du Pré.

Harvey shook his head.

"I just want to know if any of them do."

"Okay," said Du Pré.

"*Any* of them," said Harvey.

"You boys," said Madelaine, "you have time, compare your

secret decoder rings, that shit, me, I take this Blackfeet, we go dance."

Harvey got up and he took off his overcoat and put it on a hook. He followed Madelaine back out.

The jukebox fired up.

Some cheers.

Harvey was a very good dancer. Du Pré wasn't.

He stared at the photographs.

They look different now anyway.

Shit.

That Harvey, don't tell me shit.

I am tired, this.

Du Pré got up and he slid the photographs together and then he put them in the pocket of Harvey's overcoat and he picked up his drink and he walked out into the bar.

Harvey and Madelaine were dancing, some sort of cross between square dancing and mud wrestling.

Du Pré got another drink and he went round the bar and sat by Bart. Bart was clapping and cheering and whistling.

Madelaine and Harvey stopped when the music did. They bowed.

Everyone cheered and clapped.

"They're good!" said Bart.

Du Pré grinned. Madelaine came over to him and kissed him on the forehead.

"Damn Harvey still don't ask me to run off with him," she said.

The telephone rang. Susan Klein answered and listened for a moment and then she brought the telephone over to Du Pré.

Du Pré looked at it before he picked it up.

"Gabriel," said Benny Klein, "I'm out on the road front of the Messmer place. Got a killing."

Du Pré waited.

"You know who?" he asked.

"That bastard Messmer," said Benny. "Looks like somebody gave him both barrels. Cut him in half, I think."

Du Pré nodded.

He listened to Benny retch on the other end of the line.

❖ CHAPTER 13 ❖

There were a lot of people standing around the SUV with the blown-out window and the blood splashed in sheets on the passenger side glass.

The driver's door was open and what was left of Messmer lay like a pile of dirty laundry, here and there.

Benny Klein was sitting in his police cruiser, legs out the door and head down between his knees.

A few Siberian elms sat beside an irrigation ditch, close enough to the road so that anyone with a grain of sense would slow and stop to look to their right before pulling out on the county road.

Some tall weeds stood in the barrow pit.

Du Pré nodded and he flicked on his flashlight and went to the weeds. Lots of shoes had been through the weeds.

There is where I would wait, Du Pré thought, wait for him, look to his right there, step up and forward and pull the trigger. Good range for a sawed-off shotgun, about ten feet.

Du Pré knelt and he stared and he lifted up the ground with his eyes and he spun it. He set his flashlight down so the beam played at a stiff angle to the surface.

There. Son of a bitch.

The cross-stitch pattern in a little mud. Stand up, right-footed, roll a little to the left, there it is.

So the guy with the shotgun is wearing moccasins.

Lots of people here wear moccasins. Centuries they wear moccasins. Catfoot wears moccasins. All the people wear moccasins are dead. Pelon wears moccasins. Benetsee wears running shoes, kind with the Velcro strips for shoelaces.

Pelon is gone north. Also he is just not the kind of guy waits in the bushes, kill somebody with a shotgun. Benetsee don't send him, anyway. Benetsee send me he send anyone.

Shit.

Ver' nice.

Harvey is lying to me, but he is a poor liar, so I know pret' soon what he wants, or maybe he is a good liar and I am a fool. Can't get in the damn door, send Du Pré through the window.

My head it aches.

Du Pré went to his cruiser and got in and he fished the bottle of whiskey out from under the seat and he had some. He rolled a smoke and lit it with the shepherd's lighter his daughter Maria had sent him from Spain.

Benetsee tell me, Okay, Du Pré, this is a bad one, you figure it out.

I want to take my grandchildren fishing. Reservoir, throw them worms out, get a bunch of perch. Perch are good eating, not like them damn trout.

The people milling around the SUV broke up into little groups.

Two of them were the hands Du Pré had seen at the cattle shipping.

This goddamn crap is like a bad toothache coming on, it will not go away, and it is my tooth.

Harvey walked over to Du Pré's car. He bent down so he could speak through the open window.

"You see anything?" he said.

"What is that stuff they do, the city?" said Du Pré. "That break dancing like on the television. The shooter he is over there in the weeds, these people break dance over there. Do it a long time, too, them big dumb shoes they wear."

"I know," said Harvey. "They're, uh, Drug Enforcement."

"Somebody shoot that asshole I don't give a shit," said Du Pré.

"His parents, the Messmers," said Harvey, "front-end blowout on their motor home. New tires. Less than ten thousand miles on them. Best grade. They stopped for coffee at a roadhouse, you know, two-lane road. We think the tire that blew was the left front one, it burned in the wreck. The lab guys worked on it a while. They couldn't find anything, really, but when the techs looked at the tire marks on the road, it seemed that the left front one just sort of blew, like that. It was there and then it wasn't."

So somebody fuck with the tire, Du Pré thought. His head hurt.

"They'll send somebody new, Gabriel," said Harvey. "I am just as interested."

Du Pré nodded.

Harvey looked over at the SUV.

"Maybe they already did," said Du Pré.

"Nah," said Harvey, "they put a couple twenty-two hollow points in your brain when they demote you. Usually your best friend does it, they do try to spare people's feelings."

"Who are these bastards?" asked Du Pré.

Harvey sighed.

"Real bastards," he said. "Very smart. Perfectly legitimate businesses, real estate, a couple resorts, trucking, and the illegal stuff is very carefully kept apart. No one who hasn't committed murder is a member. They are so modern they give extensive psychological tests to all employees, pure sociopath is the only passing grade. Makes it kinda difficult to stick an agent in. We test, too, hoping for other things, you know."

Du Pré laughed. His headache was fading.

"Someday maybe you tell me things," Du Pré said, "now you just tell me some of them. I look around when I am there, I don't do no more."

Harvey nodded.

"Yeah," he said, "like you tell me everything."

Tell you everything I be in that Walla Walla prison, the rest of my life, Du Pré thought.

My head aches.

An ambulance was coming up the road, blue lights and red lights and yellow lights flashing.

"Poor Benny," said Harvey. "He's still puking."

Harvey stood up. He walked away.

The ambulance backed up to the SUV with the dead man in it and a couple men got out and began to put on white plastic suits. Then they slid and tugged Messmer out of the SUV on to an open body bag and they zipped the bag up and sluiced it down with a hose and nozzle from a tank of something. They shut the door of the SUV and then put yellow tape on the seams of the doors on both sides. A big yellow sticker on the side panels.

The men were so bloody, red on white, that they looked like butchers.

They hosed each other down and then took off the suits and carefully put them in a bag and sealed it and then bagged the surgical gloves that they were wearing.

Scared of him he is dead, Du Pré thought, got that AIDS, maybe he got something that is worse.

Me, I don't want none of this.

But I got it. Benetsee give it to me. He say, here, Du Pré, is big pile of shit, all yours.

Du Pré had some more whiskey. He rolled another smoke.

A bullbat clacked past overhead.

Early for him come north.

Take everybody, go north, too, Canada, play my fiddle. We live in teepees a while.

Du Pré got out of the car and he walked to the fence around the big pasture and he went through the barbed wire and over to the little irrigation ditch that carried water to a hayfield across the road and down a good ten feet in elevation. The Siberian elms were in first bud. Du Pré stepped across the ditch and he walked down a deer path by the water and then out through another fence that ran parallel to the road. He flicked on his flashlight.

The car or little truck had been parked on dry gravel, ricked up by the snowplows in the winter. He followed the depressions to the hardpan surface of the road.

Tell that it was here and went there but there have been other cars past now and there is nothing but the little dents, the gravel.

He went back to where the car or light truck had sat.

Du Pré cast the light back and forth, back and forth.

Something tiny and red. Sitting on a small flat stone.

Du Pré bent down and he stared.

A bead. Just a little red bead, hardly bigger than a pinhead.

He fumbled in his pocket for his bifocals.

Damn eyes go. My dick is next. Shit.

Du Pré got down on his hands and knees. He picked up the bead and put it in his mouth. He lifted up the small flat stone. He began to carefully lift up pieces of gravel.

Nothing.

Feet on the gravel. Du Pré looked over.

Wingtips.

"Find something?" said a voice Du Pré didn't know.

"Lost my contact lens," said Du Pré, not looking up.

The feet crunched away. In a moment Du Pré heard a car coming toward him. He looked until the doors slammed.

Du Pré got up and looked at them.

"Good place for that break dancing," he said.

He walked back toward his cruiser.

❧ CHAPTER 14 ❧

D u Pré looked over the shipping receipts, bills of sale, and the certificates of vaccination. He nodded and scribbled awhile on the forms. The drivers of the haulers backed them up to the loading chute, a small mound with a fence and a gate halfway up the drive to the main house, and then they opened the rear doors and the horses began to back out.

The horses were dizzy and sick and confused from the trip. They walked very slowly and bit halfheartedly at each other.

"Roddy took the call, there's some manager feller coming, said he'd be here today sometime," said the hand. His name was Bill.

"Sure a damn shame that Messmer was shot," said Du Pré.

Bill snorted and walked off toward the pasture.

Du Pré ambled back to the old cruiser. Madelaine was sitting in it, racking beads on a needle and dropping them on to a thread. She would get the number she wanted and then she would tie the thread off.

Du Pré put his notebook with the numbers from the vaccination certificates in the glove box.

"That is all, Du Pré?" she said.

"Yeah," said Du Pré. "That Bill said some manager is coming. So we don't know much and got no reason to stay."

"One of them guys don't shoot him?" said Madelaine. She nodded at the two hands in the pasture.

Du Pré shook his head. They could have, maybe, but they didn't. Cowboys hate a boss they go. Not a killing matter.

Du Pré started the old car with the very new engine and turned around and headed back down to the county road.

"There?" said Madelaine, when they passed the spot where Messmer had been shot. A few crumbs of glass glinted in the road.

Du Pré nodded.

"You are sad some these days, Du Pré," said Madelaine.

Du Pré grunted.

"Used to be quiet here, not like this," said Madelaine. "You maybe tell that damn Harvey to fuck himself; you know, you don't owe him nothin'."

Du Pré gunned the engine and flew down the gravel road.

The sun was flaming on the peaks of the Wolf Mountains, thick with snow. The creeks were running deep and muddy and the real runoff hadn't even begun. New grass lifted green where the sun lingered on the fields. The mule deer looked thin and scabby, still starving. Some were pulling at a haystack.

"It is mine," said Du Pré. He pulled over on a snowplow turnout.

"Long time," said Madelaine, "them young Métis had good eyes, they spend their time out watching, looking for the enemies coming. White men give us glasses and you still looking, Du Pré, out there."

Du Pré nodded.

You kick my ass I don't.

"Look for your people, Du Pré," said Madelaine. "Harvey is just a damn Blackfeet anyway."

Du Pré laughed. He roared.

One time Métis' come back, got scalps, priest complain, say

that is not right. Métis' woman grab priest by the balls. She say, you, you got no children, priest, what are these for? Our men take scalps, for our children. They are Métis' scalps, we get them back.

Priest take his wounded nuts to Montréal, complain. They send us a new priest, he don't have a word to say, scalps.

Funny song.

Du Pré hummed it and then he sang a little and Madelaine joined him.

Long time gone.

"You tell that Harvey that," he said.

"Me I will," said Madelaine. "Grab his nuts while I talk, so he listen."

"He is lost," said Du Pré.

"Yah," said Madelaine.

"FBI they are very good, cities," said Du Pré. "Even they are looking at that crazy bomber, his cabin, some can hide, sleep out in the winter. But there is no place here. No cowboys in that FBI."

"Screw that Harvey," said Madelaine. "My Du Pré he got them good eyes."

Du Pré looked at her.

"I am scared, me," said Madelaine.

Du Pré waited.

"What they do here is bad but we don't know," said Madelaine. "I will be better I know."

Du Pré waited.

"We go and get some pink wine, maybe some prime rib," said Madelaine.

It was Friday.

Us good Catholics always eat that prime rib on Friday.

Du Pré nodded and he drove on.

They stopped at Madelaine's and she went in for a moment

while Du Pré smoked and waited. She wasn't gone long and when she came out she had on a red silk blouse and silver and turquoise jewelry and a concho belt and tight black jeans and high tooled boots.

Ver' pretty woman, Du Pré thought.

We are lucky, us.

The bar was filling up and Susan Klein was dashing around and three other women who worked there weekends were cooking and bartending and waiting on the tables.

They waited in line behind some other couples, ranchers and their wives, one family of six.

Susan put them at a table near the bar.

"It get bad, I help," said Madelaine.

She went off to pour their drinks. She came back.

She had a tall glass of pink wine, whiskey for Du Pré, a little plate of cheese and elk sausage and crackers.

Their meals came quickly.

Du Pré looked at the big slab of rare meat swimming in juices. He shook a lot of salt on it and added pepper and then he cut it with his fork. Susan still had the meat cooler in the back and the cuts of prime rib hung till they had black beards of mold four inches long and when the mold was cut off there was fat white as ivory. Someone who had once owned the saloon knew meat.

They ate and when they were through Madelaine took the dishes back and Du Pré mopped off the table and set it up for the next customers.

He went to the bar and sat all the way at the end, nursing his drink. Bart and Booger Tom came in and sat with him. No one had a damn thing to say.

The owl with the camera in its eye sat still, like it was hunting.

"Harvey left," said Bart, "just like that."

Du Pré nodded.

Booger Tom held out his worn old hand and Du Pré rolled him a smoke.

Bassman and Père Godin came in dragging the amplifiers and instrument cases.

Du Pré started. He had forgotten that they were to play.

Like some poison in the air, he thought, everything is different but no reason why.

Bassman had the same burlap blonde with him he'd had the last time. She'd lasted well, over a month. More nonreturnable than most.

Du Pré got his fiddle from the trunk of the cruiser and he took it in and set it behind the bar on a small shelf to warm up so it would not go out of tune when he began to play. It would anyway.

I don't feel like playing, Du Pré thought. I play but I am somewhere else.

He had a couple more drinks. Père Godin set notes with the accordion and Du Pré and Bassman tuned to him. The old man had a new gold tooth right in the top front rank of his mouth. He smiled a lot. The lights danced off it.

Du Pré started to play but he felt leaden and the music would go along like a sulky horse but he couldn't find a way to make it rise and run.

Some times are like this, not good, you just get through them.

The crowed was thin and polite.

Du Pré and Bassman and Père Godin did a set and they put down their instruments and Bassman nodded to Du Pré.

"Take a long break, Du Pré," he said. "Everybody's mind is somewhere else. Mine too, me, I don't know where but it is gone."

Du Pré nodded.

Père Godin went off with his gold tooth blazing, looking for another woman to charm and have his babies. He had seventy children, more.

Du Pré shrugged.

Bart and Booger Tom were sitting together and not even insulting each other.

Du Pré sat and had a long drink and then another. Madelaine was back in the kitchen, cooking.

The band went back to the stage and they played on in the dead night.

Damn prime rib didn't even taste that good, Du Pré thought.

♣ CHAPTER 15 ♣

Though whoever pulled the plug on Brother Larry committed a bad, nasty, unlawful, horrible act for which I would of course like to see the perpetrator get life in the slam, if you run on to them give them my thanks and don't tell me who it is," said Harvey Wallace.

Du Pré didn't say anything.

"So that was it? The horses come and the hands stay on?" said Harvey.

"Yah," said Du Pré.

"Okay," said Harvey, "look, anyone comes to run that place I would like a photograph pronto."

"Yah," said Du Pré. "Send one of your photographers, wingtips, I see he gets an appointment."

"All that lives in Cooper County comes to the Toussaint Saloon," said Harvey, "I think."

"Yah," said Du Pré.

"You know," said Harvey, "I would rather talk to Madelaine. She talks back. Not that everything she has to say is exactly pleasant, but I have an actual feeling that communication is happening. Big thing in the eighties you remember, lots of books. Courses at motels."

Du Pré handed the phone to Madelaine.

The bar was nearly empty. The day was gray and mean.

Du Pré rolled a smoke and lit it. He sipped some of his whiskey ditch.

"Yah," said Madelaine into the telephone. She lifted it from her ear and she made a face at Du Pré.

"You are ver' cranky, Harvey," she said. "I maybe call your wife, tell her she don't have to put up with your crap."

Madelaine laughed and hung the telephone back up.

"Sun comes out sometime," she said to Du Pré, "someone tell you a joke you never heard before. It will happen, Du Pré. You guys, never did believe, tomorrow."

Du Pré snorted.

The door opened and a young cowboy came in, wearing a brand-new yellow slicker. His hat was clean and blocked and hadn't seen much by way of weather. His boots were handmades, from a good boot maker.

The young cowboy walked quickly to the bar and he slipped up on a stool and he nodded pleasantly and tipped his hat to Madelaine. He fished a bill out of his shirt pocket and he put it on the bartop.

Susan Klein was back in the kitchen.

Madelaine got up and went through the lift board and down the bar.

"A draft, ma'am," said the young cowboy.

Madelaine drew a schooner and she set it in front of the cowboy.

"I don't see you before," she said. "You are working here?"

"Yes, ma'am," said the young cowboy. His voice was soft and Southern. "I work for the Martins."

Du Pré looked over.

The young cowboy looked at Du Pré levelly. He had a square face and bright blue eyes and brown hair cut short, and sideburns.

Du Pré nodded to him.

Martins they got a ver' big spread. Also two of them are dead, that wolf crap a few years ago, tough people those Martins, they die pret' good.

Old lady she is still ver' much alive, her grandkids, they are about grown now, the oldest ones.

"I was at school with Paul Martin," said the young cowboy, "so I thought I'd ride for a couple of years before I get on with my life."

Du Pré nodded.

Kid is too big to be a hand long, Du Pré thought, a riding one.

"You must be Gabriel Du Pré," said the young cowboy.

"Yah," said Du Pré, "I am him."

"I look forward to your music," said the young cowboy. His soft Southern voice had a faint lisp, a whistle almost too soft to hear.

"I am Madelaine," said Madelaine. She held out her hand. The young cowboy took it.

"Jerry," said the young cowboy, "Jerry Jacquot. Jeremiah, actually, big name in the seventies, like Kimberley for girls."

He drank his beer.

Madelaine drew him another and she made change and left it by the ashtray. She came back around and she sat by Du Pré.

Jerry got up and he went over to the pool table and he took his slicker and hat off and put them on the pegs in the wall, then he put a quarter in the plunger and pushed it in and the balls racketed down to the end. He fished them out in double handfuls and put them in the rack and positioned the balls and lifted the rack and slid it back in its slot. He went to the cue rack and found one he liked and then he sipped from his schooner of beer.

"You play, Mr. Du Pré?" he asked.

Du Pré shook his head.

"Me, I do," said Madelaine. "Du Pré he is not much fun."

They flipped for the break and Jerry made it. No balls fell.

Madelaine took an easy straight shot with a solid-color ball and she made two more before missing a long bank shot.

Jerry made one and then he looked around the table, spotted an easy shot, and sent a stripe into a corner pocket.

He blew the next shot.

Pool is a boring business, Du Pré thought. I hate card games too.

Click clack thump.

Madelaine made a couple more, Jerry a couple more.

They were down to one each and the eight ball.

Madelaine made hers and she frowned. The eight ball was a hard shot, it would have to be barely touched by the cue ball to roll into the corner pocket. She hit the cue ball a little too hard and her solid red ball bounced off the corner of the bumper and moved out to the middle of the table.

Jerry missed his shot. Easy shot, too.

Madelaine made hers this time and then she knocked in the eight.

Jerry put in another quarter.

A couple middle-aged ranchers came in, red-cheeked and laughing. One had sold something to the other.

They bought whiskey ditches and went over to watch Madelaine and Jerry.

The ranchers began to argue. Finally one bet the other, that Madelaine would beat the kid's ass. Twenty bucks.

Madelaine beat the kid's ass.

"Over my head," said Jerry Jacquot, coming back to the bar with his empty schooner.

The ranchers argued about who shot pool best and they squared off and laid bills on the table.

Jerry Jacquot got another schooner of beer and he munched potato chips.

Madelaine stood behind the bar. One or another of the ranchers would come and she would refill their glasses. They were drinking a fair amount even for ranchers.

Jerry Jacquot wrote in a notebook, a brown leather one, medium-sized, with a snap to hold it shut.

One of the ranchers whooped.

"All for you!" he roared.

The defeated man came to the bar with the glasses.

Madelaine took the old ones and put them in the sink and she got new glasses and ice and whiskey and water. She pushed them over and waved away the money.

"I got fifty bucks says I can beat him," said Jerry Jacquot. He took a fifty-dollar bill out of his shirt pocket.

The rancher and Jerry Jacquot went back to the table.

"He is going, take their money," said Madelaine.

"Uh," said Du Pré.

"All the time he is playing me," said Madelaine, "he is dogging it. Harder to make bad shots almost good than it is make good shots."

The balls rumbled down the table's guts.

Du Pré laughed.

Susan Klein came out of the kitchen. With her free hand she shoved some of her hair under the scarf she wore. She set some chicken wings in front of Du Pré.

"Try 'em," she said.

"These are not the frozen ones with the sauce already on," said Madelaine.

Du Pré munched hot chicken wings and he had a couple schooners of beer with them. They were very good.

He looked over at the pool table.

There was serious money on the rail. Hundred-dollar bills.
Jerry Jacquot smiled.

He had white even teeth, straight and brilliant.

"He go to that Yale," said Madelaine.

Du Pré nodded and had another chicken wing.

✦ CHAPTER 16 ✦

Du Pré parked in front of the little stone stuck on the side of the bar where the Cooper County Museum was. He got out and the kids in the back seat scrambled through the doors.

Miss Porterfield stood at the entrance, beaming.

They leave a goddamn smoking ruin, Du Pré thought, little heathens.

Why don't you take some kids, the museum, said Madelaine. Me, I help Jacqueline here. You be a grandfather.

Me, I find a nice rock, the ocean, sit there, drink whiskey, eat seals. Play my fiddle good, them yachts come bust up on the rocks. I do all right.

When the kids got to the entrance and Miss Porterfield they got very quiet and respectful.

"Now children," said Miss Porterfield, "please do not touch the things in the museum without asking me if it is all right."

Ver' good, Du Pré thought, they don't behave, they don't get them buffalo rifles, blow out windows at three miles. Me, I fire one of them .45-120's once, got a shell big as a damn cigar. I am small, it knock me fifteen feet. Catfoot he come home, look at the old buffalo rifle, look at me, don't say nothing. Just shake his head.

"You clean that?" says my Papa Catfoot. I say "Yes." "Good," he say, "it rusts easy."

Long time gone.

90

Du Pré went in and he looked at the few exhibits and he looked through the entryway to the bar. Velma was there.

"Why don't you go and have a nice drink, Gabriel?" said Miss Porterfield.

Du Pré nodded.

Look at this dress! A doll got a porcelain head, it says! Any bullets for the buffalo rifle?

Grandson, that one, Du Pré thought.

He went on in. Velma had a tall ditch ready for him by the time he got there.

"Monster herding," she said. "I expect you would rather be out there inspectin' brands."

"Yah," said Du Pré.

"Funny about Messmer getting killed," said Velma, "I mean blown in half, I hear. He was a bastard."

Du Pré looked at her.

"We was in the same class," said Velma. "He was one mean kid."

Du Pré nodded. He sipped some of his drink.

Miss Porterfield was talking. The children laughed and laughed. She came in to the bar.

Velma heated a brandy snifter and she put a good shot in it and slid it over.

Miss Porterfield got up on the stool, grabbing on to the back. Her legs were short and she had to step on to the boot rest to slide on to the seat.

Not much bigger than the kids she teach, Du Pré thought, she seem plenty big to me.

Quiet them little heathens down right now.

"Marvelous children," said Miss Porterfield. She sipped her brandy.

"I was talkin' to Du Pré about Larry Messmer," said Velma.

Miss Porterfield nodded.

"Yes," she said, "quite strange, really. You know, Du Pré, that old Albert Messmer died the same way?"

Du Pré looked at her.

"Right out back of here," she said. "The saloons had no plumbing, of course, and so there were outhouses in the back of the lot. More than one shooting. Messmer was probably involved in one, before he was killed, that is."

Du Pré sipped his drink.

"Messmer and a man named Cunningham both took a fancy to a whore named Shot Glass Lulu," said Miss Porterfield, "and one night in 1881 Cunningham waited out by the outhouse for Messmer. Cunningham had a pistol. But Messmer had a sawed-off shotgun. Cunningham shot Messmer in the thigh, but Messmer shot Cunningham in the face, from the side, I guess, anyway. Blew off the man's nose and lips. Cunningham lived, which is odd, since face wounds infect so readily, and he was known, of course, as the Man With No Face—sounds like a bad Italian western— and Cunningham moved down someplace in Wyoming and he never came back here."

One of the kids hollered in the museum.

Du Pré looked over.

Miss Porterfield chuckled.

"I put some batteries and lights in the stereopticon," she said. "I rewired it, and the children are just looking at three-dimensional photographs of Yellowstone Park."

Du Pré nodded. He remembered the strange old thing, a frame that held two photographs carefully lined up behind little panes of thin glass, and a pair of strange binoculars to look at them through.

"Anyway," said Miss Porterfield, "much, much later, in 1898,

Albert Messmer went out to the outhouse and someone shot him with a shotgun and tore him half in two."

Du Pré nodded.

"You know what happen, his Métis children?" said Du Pré.

Miss Porterfield shook her head.

"So many of the early settlers just gave their Indian wives the boot, along with the children of the marriage, when a white wife was on the way, usually. I have no idea where they may have gone. The wife was Shoshone, I believe, but the Shoshones were a long way from here. I would think they would go to the Red River country."

Du Pré nodded.

Songs about that, how the Métis took in the poor wives and children when the white men didn't want them anymore. When the trains come, the song went, the breeds go back to the teepees. Métis teepees, like the other Plains people, but we got them carts, too, lots of pictures of them teepees and the carts.

"No one was ever arrested and tried for Albert Messmer's murder," said Miss Porterfield. "I saw Benny Klein and asked him when he was going to get around to doing that. Poor Benny."

Yah, Du Pré thought, poor Benny he think it maybe happen the week before he is Sheriff, not one hundred years ago.

Long time gone.

Miss Porterfield finished her brandy and she held out her glass and Velma put in some more. They locked glances, and Velma tipped the bottle again, another splash.

"I have the files from back then," said Miss Porterfield.

Du Pré nodded.

Got no files, us Métis, we don't break the law because we do we get sent back, Canada, thrown in prison, and we can't write so we got nothing for the museum.

I got them songs, though.

Miss Porterfield gulped her brandy and walked toward the entrance to the little museum.

Du Pré looked at Velma.

"She drinks too much," said Velma. "So do you, so do I."

Velma reached down and lifted up a pint and sipped something.

"She's real lonely," said Velma. "I wish she could a taught till she dropped dead. We all had her for class, right, Du Pré. Right?"

Du Pré nodded.

The sound of a music box tinkled from the museum.

Du Pré went over and he stood in the door.

The music box was enormous, the size of a flat steamer trunk. The lid stood open, and behind glass little figurines played out a Punch and Judy show, the spectators shaking their heads.

In the open trunk little ballerinas pirouetted across painted glass.

A circular brass shield slid into the floor and a tiny orchestra rose up.

Du Pré's grandchildren watched as enchanted as children dead for fifty years had.

Not like them damn TV games, the computers.

Du Pré hated television, video games, and most of the rest of the twentieth century. He doubted he would like the twenty-first much better.

The music box tinkled.

The children stared.

Miss Porterfield looked down. Her face was sad and smooth and lost.

The ballerinas bowed.

The little orchestra dropped through the floor.

Miss Porterfield reached for the key and she rewound the music box and it began to play again.

The grandchildren looked at Du Pré.

He nodded and they followed him out.

Miss Porterfield didn't look up.

The music box played on.

✤ CHAPTER 17 ✤

Du Pré pulled up in the rutted drive that led to Benetsee's cabin just as the sun slid down behind the rise of the High Plains to the west. He shut the engine off and he sat there smoking for a moment. The glass cooled, cold was sliding down like a blanket off shoulders from the Wolf Mountains. It would freeze before midnight.

Du Pré got out. He walked around the dead cabin, to the sweat lodge, reeking of mildew. The stump halfway to the creek had an empty gallon jug on it, the cheap wine Benetsee drank.

Du Pré put it on the ground and he sat. The wood was damp and cold against his ass.

I know this old man forty years and I think he is just some old fool drunk. He help me find things I knew were there, without him I don't find them, don't know my people. He help me plenty.

He is gone.

Du Pré, you figure this out.

Everything is dark, I can't see, but I am afraid, so far of nothing. Madelaine is afraid.

Ever'body afraid of the dark. You can't see.

"Damn you!" Du Pré yelled.

The night ate his scream.

Gone, I need you and you are gone. Damn old man.

I cannot see this.

Messmer is dead. The bad guy, somebody kill him, what next?

He got up and he walked down by the creek, the deep pool Benetsee jumped in after sweating, cold clear water eight feet deep. The water weeds danced, dark against the pale gravels.

He was cold. He went back to his old cruiser. He turned on the engine and the heater and he sat there with the window open halfway.

A loud thump next to his left ear, something tickled his nose. Du Pré reached for the dash and he flicked on the dome light.

Feathers. Soft gray feathers, down floating.

Something flopped on the ground.

Du Pré opened the door.

A Great Horned Owl lay on its back, talons up and clasping, wings spread and shivering.

Du Pré waited. The owl struggled for a moment and then managed to get upright. It fell.

Du Pré reached in back and got his old roughout jacket and he dropped it over the owl and rolled the leather tight around the bird. He dumped out the few things in the cooler and laid the jacket and the prisoner in it.

He drove off. In Cooper he called the vet and met him at the clinic. The vet was new, in his fifties, moved from Great Falls when his sons were licensed and took over the business. He was a homesteader's grandson named Drewer.

The vet carefully unwrapped the owl. The big bird blinked, the black pupils in the yellow eyes huge. The vet grabbed the bird and he put him on a T-stand in the corner. The owl kept twisting his head.

The vet took a penlight from his pocket, held it close to the bird's left eye, and flicked it on. The bird did not flinch and the pupil did not react. The vet did the same thing to the right eye.

"He's blind," said the vet.

Blind owl don't last too long out there, Du Pré thought.

"About all we could hope for is sending him to a zoo," said the vet.

Du Pré looked at the floor.

"I got grandkids," he said finally, " 'bout time they learned about the birds. They take care of him."

"Okay," said the vet, "but you know this big guy will make very short work of a cat."

Du Pré nodded.

Long time gone Catfoot had found a Great Gray Owl with a bad wing and brought him home. The owl got well, soon enough, and left, but it came back every so often for a while.

One day Du Pré saw the huge owl skim over a neighbor's woodpile, and grab something, and when the owl got close Du Pré saw the tail of the cat hanging down, fluttering like a hairy windsock.

The huge owl sat on the corral pole by the gate and ate the cat.

The neighbor asked if Du Pré had seen it.

My cat, the big one?

No.

I did not see your cat.

"Otherwise the owl seems fine," said the vet. "I expect one or another of your grandkids will find out owls are nothing to mess with."

"Yah," said Du Pré, offering the vet a couple of twenties.

"Buy me a drink sometime," said the vet. "Happy to help."

Du Pré went out with the owl wrapped in the jacket and sitting in the cooler.

Jacqueline opened the front door of her house, Du Pré's house, Catfoot's house. She had heard his car pull in.

"Brought you an owl," said Du Pré.

Jacqueline looked at him.

"Sure," she said.

Du Pré carried the cooler to the sunporch and he lifted out the owl and he unwrapped it and set it on the back of a rocking chair. The owl stood still, only the head moving.

"It is blind, him," said Du Pré.

"Oh," said Jacqueline, "the poor thing." She clasped her hands.

Du Pré smiled. That is the best-off owl, Montana, it just don't know it yet.

"The kids asleep?" said Du Pré.

Jacqueline nodded.

"Raymond he is sleeping, too," she said. "He sleep a lot, healing up."

"Him got to have fur and bones, what he eats," said Du Pré.

"Tomorrow," said Jacqueline, "I will turn my kids, trappers, feed the owl. Tonight he get meatballs. I got some left over."

She went off to the kitchen. Du Pré heard the refigerator door open.

Jacqueline came back, carrying a plastic container. She fished a meatball out on a fork and held it in front of the bird's beak. The owl blinked, raised a foot, grabbed the meatball, and began to eat.

"Him like Italian," said Jacqueline. "Where you get him?"

"Fly into my car window, Benetsee's," said Du Pré.

Jacqueline crossed herself.

The owl finished the meatball. She held out another.

Du Pré waited while his daughter fed the owl. Four meatballs. It ignored a fifth.

The owl ruffled its feathers and then it crapped.

Du Pré went and got paper towels and a soapy sponge and he cleaned the mess up.

Jacqueline made tea.

My beautiful daughter, Du Pré thought, twelve kids and she look about eighteen.

He remembered her mother, dead over twenty years now.

Long time gone.

"Raymond, he goes back to Billings in a week," said Jacqueline, "Get some casts off."

"I drive him," said Du Pré.

"Thank you, Papa," she said. "You are a good Papa, stay here with these kids he is in the hospital. I know you are not good with kids. Think they break or something."

Du Pré laughed.

My wife die I have little daughters, they take care of me. One have twelve kids, the other is gone, she won't come back here. Not Maria.

"You see anything, Benetsee's?" said Jacqueline.

Du Pré shook his head.

"Him, Pelon are gone."

"Madelaine she is worried about something," said Jacqueline. "You know what it is she worries?"

The dark, she worries.

Me, too.

"No," said Du Pré.

There was a sudden screech from the sunporch, a cat surprised. The scream choked off.

"Shit," said Jacqueline. "The kids, they let that cat in. It is to be outside, that cat. No cats in the house."

They walked back to the sunporch.

The owl was standing on a tortoise-shell cat's body.

"Well," said Jacqueline, "him got fur and bones, eat now."

Du Pré laughed.

"This works good," said Jacqueline. "Kids keep the cats out now, the owl eats them."

"I go now," said Du Pré.

The owl ripped a strip of skin and fur off the dead cat with one pull of its beak.

"I let you know what the kids name it," said Jacqueline.

Du Pré nodded and went out.

✤ CHAPTER 18 ✤

I got to take a prisoner down and bring one back," said Benny Klein, "and the other guys are stuck, got a domestic violence and a burglary. You wouldn't mind I would appreciate it."

"Yah," said Du Pré.

"Well," said Benny, "since you're brand inspectin' again, at least this is about horses."

"Somebody cut the fence at the Messmers," said Du Pré, "and the horses get out."

Put a hole in a fence, animals will find it.

Catfoot tries to raise goats, once, says he learn a fence will hold a goat if it will hold water, too.

"Thanks," said Benny.

"Du Pré," said Madelaine, "your eggs, chilies will get cold, you eat."

Du Pré sat down and he ate his breakfast. He drank coffee and then he rolled a cigarette and another for Madelaine. She had one after breakfast, and no more the rest of the day, unless she drank pink bubbly wine.

"Who cut the Messmers' fence?" asked Madelaine. "They are all dead anyway."

Du Pré nodded.

Yah.

He drank the last of the coffee and he got up and he went out to his cruiser and he got a scraper and started in on the frost thick on the glass. Finally he started the engine and turned on the heater high and he went back in for another cup of coffee.

"Them cowboys run them horses back in by now," said Madelaine, "so why you go anyway?"

"I tell that Benny I do that," said Du Pré.

Madelaine nodded.

She was some crabby this morning.

Du Pré had his coffee and by the time he went back out the frost had fallen off.

He drove off toward the bench road.

The road was slick with frost and Du Pré could drive only about forty. It took half an hour to get close to the Messmers' place. He came over a hill and saw the horses streaming back up the road, the two hands trotting along behind.

A couple people blocked the road by the hole in the fence. The horses slowed and milled and then one dashed through the hole and the others followed.

By the time Du Pré pulled up and parked the two hands were down on the ground stretching the wire back. The fencing was pretty new and most of the posts were steel.

Du Pré got out and he walked over by the fence. The ground had been pounded by the horse's hooves. The fence had been under good tension. One snip and the wire would pull the ties off for three or four posts in each direction.

Four strands. Take about one minute.

"Stock's all here," said Roddy. He was clamping a strand of wire.

"Too early for tourists," said Bill.

"Just up and cut the fence," said Roddy. "Seems dumb you don't want to steal anything."

"Who is up there?" asked Du Pré, nodding toward the ranch buildings.

"Nobody," said Roddy. "There's supposed to be a manager comin' in today or tomorrow, and another load of horses first of next week. But it is just the two of us."

"When you find this?" said Du Pré.

"Neighbor called about two in the morning," said Roddy.

"The horses was all over hell down there in the crick bottom," said Bill. "We went out right away and tossed down hay and they came but we had to wait for first light."

"I go up there a moment," said Du Pré.

"We's told not to let no one on the place," said Roddy.

"I got to take this report," said Du Pré, "so I do it up there."

Roddy nodded and he took a tie out of his pocket and clamped the wire back to the steel post.

Du Pré drove on up to the ranch house. There was still a lot of frost, though the sun was cutting it where it reached.

Du Pré went to the front door. Locked. The porch was full of boots and coats and the storm door didn't quite fit. It stood open a good six inches.

He walked around back on the east side of the house.

The sun had scoured the frost away, except where a shadow touched.

Du Pré stopped and looked at the old machinery that had been rowed out back and off toward the metal machine shed.

A man, a good-sized man, had walked from the cover of the willows by the creek, ducked through the fence, and come up to the back porch.

Du Pré rolled a smoke and lit it and studied the prints in the frost until the sun wiped them away.

He went to the back door.

It wasn't shut all the way, stuck against the copper weather strip.

Du Pré peered through the dirty window in the door at the kitchen. Clean, a coffeemaker on the counter by the table.

Du Pré pushed the door open. It rasped on the linoleum.

He dropped to his haunches and he stared.

Guy is wearing moccasins.

Move carefully through the kitchen, the house, until he is sure he is not here.

Du Pré turned on the lights. They were cold bright fluorescents.

He went through the kitchen and out to the living room and then he opened the door on the left in the far wall.

An office.

Papers everywhere, drawers standing open. Files on the floor.

Du Pré stood there a long time.

"Du Pré," hollered Roddy, "you ain't supposed to be in there!"

"You had a damn burglar," Du Pré yelled. "You stay out there."

A door in the wall to the right led to a parlor.

Walls with old photographs, stiff-posed Messmers.

Look at that Larry Messmer, behind old Albert's beard, Du Pré thought.

Same flat cold eyes.

The room wasn't disturbed. An escritoire stood open. Du Pré looked in. Lady's paper and envelopes.

He looked at the walls.

One bare spot where a frame had once hung. Other photos of Messmers with prize bulls or beaming from behind white linen on long tables.

Du Pré walked back to the door and out into the yard.

"Burgled?" said Roddy. "They'll shitcan us for sure now."

Du Pré nodded.

He walked to his car.

✤ CHAPTER 19 ✤

I forget I have it," said Du Pré. "When I stop at that little bridge I look around some and there is this one."

Madelaine held the little plastic envelope up to the light. A red bead and a bigger brass one. She frowned.

She opened the bag and she poured the two beads out in her palm. She held the brass bead up between thumb and finger.

"Trade bead," she said, "but then all them hippies they are making those silly chokers, you can buy buffalo bone beads and solid brass ones like this. So I don't know this is a hundred years or two hundred years old or made last month, China."

Du Pré waited.

"This red bead is old, though," said Madelaine. "It is glass, but you look at it close the color is not so very even, there are rainbows in it. New ones are not like that, they are solid."

Du Pré nodded. "So the guy goes into the house his car is parked down on that bridge."

"Maybe," said Du Pré. "Maybe the guy in the house, he has a friend, be there at one time, pick him up."

"Same car?" said Madelaine.

Du Pré shrugged.

I am a good tracker, not so good as my Papa Catfoot, but pret' good, but me I don't read so good, whole horse herd goes over the top of it. Hollywood Indian can do it, but me, I cannot.

"You know," said Madelaine, "song for now is songs in the past, these people are here doin' this stuff, it has been done before."

Yah, Du Pré thought, murder and theft it is done a lot. Bible got a lot of it.

"Berne, Marisa they are riding good now," said Madelaine. "School is out maybe we go, that Canada, see our people."

Yah, Du Pré thought, you got maybe two thousand cousins up there, me, I got only about five hundred. Cousin this cousin that. Us Métis we fuck anybody.

"I put these back," said Madelaine. She gave Du Pré the beads. Du Pré looked at them.

Them don't fall off something, they fall out of the car. Loose.

Now all I got to do is figure out which person beads stuff, likes to cut guys in half, shotgun.

"How many people around here bead?" said Du Pré.

"Couple hundred," said Madelaine. "Lots of relatives come, bead. It is a big thing."

Women bead.

Hippies bead, but we don't got so many hippies.

Du Pré went out and got into his old cruiser and he drove to Cooper and parked in front of the Sheriff's office. Benny Klein's car was out front.

Du Pré went on in. He fished the little plastic envelope with the two beads in it out and he laid it on the counter. Benny was listening to someone on the phone. His eyes rolled.

"Miz Lee," he said, "I have to go. We will keep an eye out for your cat. No, I don't think your niece stole it. Yes, Miz Lee, I do have to go."

Benny put the telephone down.

"Poor old girl," he said. "Damn lonely."

"She lose her cat?" said Du Pré.

"Yeah," said Benny. "You see a tortoiseshell tom, tell him to go on home."

Her cat is eaten, that damn blind owl.

Benny looked at the beads. He looked at Du Pré.

"I find this red one, near where Messmer is shot," said Du Pré. "I find the brass one, the bridge by Messmer place, somebody cut the wire, horses get out, while the hands are chasing them, goes through the house. Looking for something, the office."

"Burgled, too?" said Benny. "That 770 Corporation is supposed to be sending a manager. Why they just don't sell the place, I don't know. For one thing, I . . . how can they own it when the damn will which would give the place to Larry ain't probated yet. Can't be. And he's dead too. The lawyers will be feedin' like maggots on that one for years."

"Who is doing the Messmers' will?" said Du Pré.

"Thought maybe you could find out," said Benny.

"I am a cow-ass man," said Du Pré. "Maybe you ask Bart to find out."

"He's got the people for it," said Benny. "Me, I'd druther go look for Miz Lee's cat."

Du Pré nodded and he left.

Beads.

He sat in his old cruiser a moment and then he drove off toward Benetsee's cabin.

It is like this whole place is covered in glue. We are talking, us, underwater. There is something but there is nothing.

He woke up when he turned into Benetsee's rutted drive, not knowing much about having got there.

The cabin was dark. The porch was wet and a raccoon had gone across it in the night.

Du Pré opened the door and looked down and saw a few damp gray feathers stuck in the grass.

The owls are blind. The raccoon is miles from where he should be. Old red trade bead at the edge of the road. Maybe it is dropped a hundred years ago, washes up, gets stuck to someone's boot, dropped in the road and the rain washes the mud away.

Maybe it don't have nothing to do with nothing.

I need Benetsee, Pelon to speak for him. Some damn thing.

A sharp crack made Du Pré jump. He looked over the hood of the cruiser. Nothing. He walked around the cabin. Nothing.

Old place, settling, something makes a noise.

Du Pré walked around behind the cabin.

He smelled smoke, dead now but made not too long ago.

He walked to the fire pit. The stones he had gathered for the old man over the years were piled neatly beside it. New wood, split to the right size, was ricked up in the pit.

Du Pré went to the cabin and he checked the back door and the little gray mess of weathered boards that worked for a stoop. A spider had built a web across the frame. Been there last time, too.

Du Pré rolled a smoke and lit it and he sat and looked up toward the butte, a three-hundred-foot-high mass of rock stuck against the foothills of the Wolf Mountains.

Du Pré started walking, up the creek to where it narrowed, jumping across and following the path through the grassy pasture and then the fence and the sage and rocks rising toward the butte.

He looked down at the path.

Moccasins. Not very long ago at that. Ten hours, twelve.

It was a good three miles to the butte. Du Pré stared at it for a long time.

Nothing. The raven that sometimes lived there was gone.

The golden eagles from the cliffs to the west were floating high, dark specks unmoving.

Who the fuck is running around here in moccasins, sweating at Benetsee's, heading for the butte?

Du Pré knelt and he looked at the tracks going up the path.

Big man, trotting, running a long distance.

He walked back toward Benetsee's cabin. He crossed the creek and he went to the lodge. The door was not where it had been. He bent and stuck his head in. The bucket and dipper were there, turned over.

Everything where it had been but not exactly.

Cuts new wood.

Got good manners.

Trots in moccasins.

What kind of moccasins?

Good ones.

Where you get good moccasins?

Same place you get those good manners.

My Papa, Catfoot, he wear them Cree moccasins all his life, hate cowboy boots, hate shoes. Walks a little pigeon-toed, like the Indians.

Du Pré laughed. He stood up.

He went out to his cruiser and got in and drove down to the road; he turned right and went along till he came to the place that the creek ran under it.

The bridge was narrow, big enough for only one truck or car at a time. There was a place to turn off on the near side.

Du Pré parked in the road and walked carefully up to the turnout.

Same little car or truck, there on the gravel, don't stay long.

Dropped off our friend.

Taxi driver pret' good, friend want to blow Messmer in half, drop him off, want to sweat, Benetsee's, drop him off.

Du Pré looked for beads but there weren't any.

❧ CHAPTER 20 ❧

The 770 Corporation owned the ranch," said Foote. "They bought it three years ago, two million. The late Messmers had the money transferred out to offshore accounts. They got four grand a month. Larry Messmer came as a manager, working for 770. If he had a will, no one knows about it."

Du Pré nodded. Lot of money.

"This 770 Corporation is where?" he said.

"California," said Foote. "Real estate mostly, some development, a large number of parking lots and Laundromats."

"They put a parking lot here, Laundromat," said Du Pré.

"No," said Foote, laughing, "but they are awfully good ways to get illegal money to look like legal money. Taken all together, they could launder a million a week without too much trouble. Hard to tell how many cars park or how many socks get washed."

"Okay," said Du Pré, "I guess that manager guy showed up, the Messmer ranch, fired the two old hands, brought some more along."

"Harvey will want to know that," said Foote. "He's in a very bad mood. If you call him, I suggest you be rude first."

Du Pré put the phone back on its hook. He turned and walked back to his stool.

Roddy and Bill were off in a corner, laughing and drinking beer. Two jobless cowboys having what fun they could.

Du Pré sipped his ditch. The bar was empty except for him and the two old hands, and Madelaine was in the kitchen with Susan Klein getting twenty big apple pies ready for the oven.

The telephone rang again.

Du Pré waited it out.

"Du Pré!" hollered Madelaine. "You pick up that phone, talk to that Harvey!"

He picked up the phone.

"Now what?" said Harvey. "What fucking godawful news have you got for me? Speak up."

Du Pré didn't say anything.

"Gabriel?" said Harvey.

"He is not here," said Du Pré. "He died, a car wreck, very sad."

"Things are not good here," said Harvey.

"Washington, D.C.," said Du Pré. "Very mean place."

"I really hate it," said Harvey, "when some asshole we are closing in on gets murdered. I really wanted to be in a room with Larry, and point out he was dead meat unless he would like to tell me lots of neat things about his best friends and then think about the witness protection program."

Du Pré snorted.

"I think I know the tracks of the guy killed him," said Du Pré. "Wears moccasins."

"The only guy in Montana who wears moccasins, I'm sure," said Harvey. "Nice slick leather soles. Not too great for identification."

"What is the 770 Corporation?" said Du Pré.

"Messmer's bunch," said Harvey. "Very well run. Accountants and lawyers stacked three deep. Very careful to obey all the laws. Very good about the environment. They do a subdivision, there is no casual destruction of the breeding grounds of the rare Left Coast Sneezing Snail. They dug up an Indian burial ground and promptly gave it back to the local Indians. 'Course the burial

112

ground was about two thousand years older than the tribe that got it, who, on the evidence, were up the coast, getting fungal infections in the British Columbia rain forest and eating a lot of banana slugs, when the Indians in the burial ground were planted, but it was great public relations."

"They got a new manager, the Messmer place," said Du Pré, "Fire the two old hands. There are some new cowboys there, not from here."

"Lou Green," said Harvey. "That's the new manager. His flunkies are from a 770 cattle ranch in Texas."

"Why are they here?" said Du Pré'.

"Well," said Harvey, "that's why I called. I thought you might know."

"Foote say the 770 Corporation it owned the Messmer place, couple years," said Du Pré. "Paid the Messmers four thousand a month."

"Yup," said Harvey. "I knew that."

"Two million," said Du Pré.

"Medium-priced ranch," said Harvey. "The money left. It's on a boat someplace."

"What you want?" asked Du Pré.

"Another life," said Harvey. "My bosses are pissing and whining about the 770 Corporation. I got so tired of it I told them that we couldn't get these guys because they are smarter than we are."

Du Pré chuckled.

"Gabriel," said Harvey, "you be careful. They are blood mad about Messmer and they want the guy did it."

Du Pré sighed.

"Why they come after me?" he said.

"It was somebody local," said Harvey. "Somebody there. We don't do that sort of thing. Messmer's pals hadn't quite decided to kill him yet, they actually liked him, one sociopath to another.

You sort of stick out. Also, there are terrible stories about you none of which I believe because if I did I would have to throw you in Walla Walla for the rest of your life."

Du Pré sipped his drink.

"Don't fuck around, me," he said. "What they maybe do."

"Wish I knew," said Harvey.

"There is a cowboy here," said Du Pré, "Jerry Jacquot, young guy. He one of your guys maybe."

"Nope," said Harvey.

"Him say he went to school, one of the Martin kids."

"Could have. Boy, I wait for the day the next generation gets pissed off there. Taylor offs himself, little brother suckers me into killing him, all over some goddamn wolves, for Chrissakes."

Du Pré waited.

"He is twenties," said Du Pré. "Said he went to that Yale."

"Okay," said Harvey. "Now, what are you gonna do about what I just told you?"

"Uh," said Du Pré.

"Gabriel," said Harvey, "this isn't funny."

"I go, talk with them," said Du Pré.

"Okay," said Harvey.

"Ask them about Messmer," said Du Pré.

"Might work," said Harvey. "Better'n them asking you, first I mean."

"You coming here?" said Du Pré.

"Sooner or later," said Harvey. "I feel I probably will."

Harvey hung up, there had been someone yelling in the background.

Madelaine came out of the kitchen. She had some smears of flour on her forehead.

"Du Pré," she said, "that Harvey he is upset."

Du Pré nodded.

"Me, I am, too," said Madelaine.

Booger Tom came in, hawking. He went back out to spit and then he came inside.

"Shit," said Booger Tom. "I feel like hell."

He had the raspy wet cough of bronchitis.

Madelaine made him a hot toddy with plenty of fresh lemon juice.

The old cowboy put some ice from Du Pré's drink in it.

He drank it down.

"Got a call from this new manager feller at the Messmer place," said Booger Tom. "Said he'd like to have me come on out and talk to him and his hands about the peculiarities of raisin' horses here."

Du Pré nodded.

Ver' smart that.

"Said I would," said Booger Tom.

Du Pré sipped his drink.

"Wanted to know should they have the brand inspector come and look at the stock. I said it didn't matter till they shipped, but if they was worried, then they ought to check their stock and if they had horses they didn't know about call you."

Du Pré nodded.

"Pleasant guy," said Booger Tom. "Very polite."

Du Pré sipped his drink.

"But after we had our little talk, he said something made me wonder," said Booger Tom.

Du Pré nodded.

"Asked me if I knew any good hands," said Booger Tom, "when I knew he'd just fired Bill and Roddy."

Du Pré looked at him.

"So I said, well, what are you lookin' for?" said Booger Tom. "Feller says just a couple good solid hands. So I says, well, you just fired 'em."

Du Pré waited.

"I had to, the guy said, too much goin' on here, the house burgled and all. I said Roddy and Bill wouldn't do no such thing. So he changes the subject, wishes me good day."

Du Pré sipped his drink.

"I go there with you," he said.

❖ CHAPTER 21 ❖

Du Pré parked next to the Messmer house and shut the engine off; he looked over at Booger Tom. The old cowboy was squinting at a memory. He was having a conversation.

Du Pré waited. Booger Tom whispered on.

The ranch manager came out, all oil and smiles. Stetson, jeans, down coat, all on a man who needed a leisure suit to be comfortable.

"Wonder how many gold chains the son of a bitch has on," said Booger Tom.

Du Pré laughed and opened the door and stood as the manager came toward him, hand outstretched.

"Good of you to come," he said. He was about forty, pale, balding, with little mean gray eyes that stayed flat while he grinned.

Booger Tom stood up on the other side of the car.

"Well," said the manager, "I'm Kelleher. Folks call me Kel." His accent was Texan, soft and round. "You're Du Pré and that's Mr. Booger Tom. Well, the boys are out in the pasture and maybe we could head out there."

Kelleher strode off and Du Pré and Booger Tom followed, slow.

By the time that they got to the pasture the four hands who had been out riding around had headed back and Kelleher stood with his hat in his hand. The wind was brisk, and he had beads of sweat on his forehead and his face was reddening.

The hands came up to the fence and got off and looped reins over the poles of the gate. They stepped through and came to Du Pré and Booger Tom and Kelleher.

"Anything you might tell us would be helpful," said Kelleher. Booger Tom shrugged.

"Bring horses in from anywhere else, keep a close eye on 'em and grain 'em good," he said. "They'll be a little sick from the travel and new grass awhile. We don't got much by way of ticks since we done shot all the Texans brung em up here. Look up there on the hills, that white band in them rocks is sulphate and them springs under it is bitter. I expect the Messmers closed 'em off, and anyway a horse would shy away from drinkin' it 'less they was real thirsty. I'd check them springs, though. Other'n that there ain't much larkspur. Little Jimson weed but not much."

The four cowboys stood looking bored.

Ride like turds hit with clubs, Du Pré thought, so this is not about horses.

"Now," said Kelleher, "how about inspecting the stock?"

Du Pré looked at him.

"You got the same twenty-three horses came," he said, "and the rest of the ranch stock. Thirty-five altogether. Same horses, last time."

Kelleher looked at him.

"That's all," he said.

Du Pré nodded.

"Well," said Booger Tom, "we got another appointment. Nice meetin' you."

They walked to the cruiser and got in and Du Pré backed and turned And he headed down to the bench road.

"Whatever the hell they are doin' there it don't have a thing to do with horses," said Booger Tom, "And if them cowboys ain't jailbirds I will eat my own dirty long johns."

118

Du Pré laughed.

"I don't mind an honest bank robber, 'cause bankers is a cause of human misery," said Booger Tom, "or a good burglar who confines his burglin' to rich folks who was too gutless to steal what they got in the first place. But them sons of bitches, whatever they is doin', are in it for the pure meanness of it all and that ain't right."

Yah, thought Du Pré, this old bastard spends time in that Deer Lodge Prison, killing a couple men. They probably needed killing. Good old Montanan, obey any law he happens to like.

"Harvey bein' like Harvey?" Booger Tom said, "wants answers but don't want to give any?"

Du Pré nodded. He rolled a smoke while they shot along the bench road.

"I got a bad feelin' about all this," said Booger Tom.

"You go shoot them all, I don't tell no one," said Du Pré.

"Been done," said Booger Tom. "They just send more."

Yah.

"Them horses is good horses," said Booger Tom, "and six of them is Thoroughbred race horses. Worth a lot of money. Now why in the hell would they put that expensive stock with them bad little cannon bones out in rough pasture like that? They'd best be back in the bluegrass, them pastures look like golf greens, ain't got a rock or a gopher hole."

Du Pré looked off the road to his left. A coyote was trotting along across a field of winter wheat. The wheat stayed bright green all through the winter, under the snow.

"Shit," said Booger Tom. "You got a rifle?"

"In the trunk," said Du Pré.

"We gotta try," said Booger Tom.

Du Pré hit the brakes just over the rise and he jumped out and opened the trunk and slid the .270 out of the case and popped the lens caps off the scopes and then trotted back to where he could see the coyote if it hadn't heard the car stop.

The coyote was just walking slowly, head down and tongue out like it was tired from running.

Du Pré laid the rifle across a fencepost and he put the crosshairs just ahead of the coyote's chest and he swung the rifle very slowly and fired, and the coyote fell over like a tin duck in a shooting gallery.

"That ain't right," said Booger Tom. "That coyote's been poisoned. Few folks are still usin' them cyanide guns but them things about drop them right there."

Du Pré nodded.

Shit, now I got to drag that fleabag son of a bitch down here, put him in the car, take him in and see. Maybe illegal poison, 1080 or thallium. Coyote come a long way from where it got poisoned, but I like to know it is being used.

Du Pré put the rifle back in the case and he locked it in the trunk and he rolled a smoke and walked back up to Booger Tom.

The old cowboy offered a short length of light rope, with a loop in one end and a big triple knot in the other.

"Drop that on a leg and jerk and run," said Booger Tom. "I'd expect you'd beat them fleas that way."

Du Pré nodded. He took the rope and went through the fence and he walked carefully across the wheat, to spare the crop.

The breeze ruffled the coyote's fur, yellow-brown and thick from winter.

Du Pré moved fast when he got near, dropping the loop over a paw and running past and jerking the animal along for fifty feet. He slid the coyote into a wide mud puddle and he waited to see if any fleas jumped off or came to the outside of the pelt.

He dragged the coyote out and put the loop over both rear feet and he walked back down through the wheat.

The dead coyote knocked over blades of wheat but they would probably recover since the pressure was slight, not as much as a boot heel.

Booger Tom waited by the cruiser.

Du Pré wrapped the coyote in a cheap blue tarp and he put it in the trunk and they drove on to Cooper. The vet was there, looking at a pair of Blue Heelers. The sheepdogs looked with utter contempt at a lady's little poodle, carefully held high away from the working classes.

"I got a coyote for you," said Du Pré. "I leave him out back. He has maybe been poisoned."

The vet nodded as the owner of the Blue Heelers led them off to have their shots.

Du Pré dumped the coyote by the back door.

Damn 1080, kill everything, coyotes, skunks and badgers and birds eat them. Got to keep them coyotes down some. Me, I don't like them poison. Old days they use that strychnine, nerve poison, put in that bad whiskey they sell the Indians. Like us Métis.

"You know that pond they made up for nothin'?" said Booger Tom.

Du Pré nodded. It was about a foot deep for most of it.

"We are thinkin' they are ignorant," said Booger Tom, "but they got to have a reason."

Du Pré nodded.

"Them's bad people," said Booger Tom.

Du Pré nodded.

"It's drugs, ain't it," said Booger Tom. "Got to be."

Du Pré shrugged. They got in the car.

"You be damn careful, Du Pré," said Booger Tom.

Du Pré looked at him.

"Them hands was takin' your size," said Booger Tom, "they was."

Du Pré started the engine.

"Du Pré," said Booger Tom sharply, "you listen up. Them hands is lookin' to kill you. They got their reasons, they are just a-waitin' on the opportunity."

Du Pré nodded.

Yah. I know.

✦ CHAPTER 22 ✦

Bassman stood out in back of the Toussaint Saloon smoking a joint the size of a rich man's cigar. The sweet smoke went down the wind. The burlap blonde had bleached her hair white and used a trowel for her eye shadow. She took a long drag on the joint and then coughed and coughed.

"She ride back with me maybe," said Bassman. "You are crazy you think she will go anyway, but I take her she wants."

Du Pré nodded.

I am worried, my Madelaine, I don't know why. The blind owl at Jacqueline's ate two more cats. Son of a bitch hears real good. Then maybe some big cat eat him. Blind owl can't tell how big something is. Me neither.

Bassman carefully clipped the coal from the end of his joint and he put it in a silver-and-turquoise case and he put the case in his pocket.

Du Pré and Bassman walked in the back door of the saloon. The burlap blonde was still coughing, holding on to the post by the Dumpster.

"They wear out," said Bassman, jerking his head at the back door.

Du Pré nodded.

I long since quit thinking about your damn women.

Père Godin was courting a young woman. The old man, white-haired, wrinkled, had so many children in so many places Madelaine said they all came home at once you would have a city.

Got to write a song about the old goat, Du Pré thought, but I don't want to hurt his feelings.

Bassman banged a tuning fork against the side of an amplifier and Du Pré adjusted the pitch of his strings, twisting the pegs and hearing the harmonics meld.

Père Godin broke off his ten thousandth seduction to come check his accordion, but it was on pitch.

"Hey," said Bassman, "we do them sound check just like the Rolling Stones."

"Who them?" said Père Godin.

"Who them?" said Père Godin, again.

"Nobody," said Bassman. "Crap rock band."

"What them need a sound check for?" said Père Godin. "If it is just rock band?"

Du Pré laughed.

Right.

It would be a couple hours before they would play. Bassman went back out to see if his burlap blonde was still alive. Père Godin went back to his ten thousandth seduction.

Du Pré took his drink back to the kitchen, where Madelaine and Susan Klein were busy feeding the seventy people sitting at tables out in the bar.

"Du Pré!" said Madelaine. "You!" She pushed a big platter with two huge prime rib roasts over the butcher-block counter toward him.

Du Pré got up and he pulled a long carving knife out of the wood block that held six. Catfoot had made them and they were black carbon steel that held an edge a long time. He had made them from some old files.

The knife was so sharp it took only three strokes to slice off each slab of prime rib, and one would have been enough but the slices had to be even, so Du Pré took care. The meat ran juices into the platter.

Madelaine brought four plates already garnished with spiced apples and horseradish and a baked potato. She forked slabs from the deck of meat on the platter and then she put a plate on each forearm and one in each hand and she was gone.

Susan Klein did the same thing.

Madelaine came back for another load.

Du Pré looked at the clock on the wall.

Them women, they feed twenty-two people, four minutes.

"Maybe you help Mrs. Steffa, the bar?" said Madelaine.

Du Pré nodded and went out. Mrs. Steffa came in once in a while, but she was a housewife instead of a barfly and her heart was not really in getting her neighbors good and drunk. It bothered her so she short-shotted them. The neighbors were too polite to complain, but they weren't happy about it either.

The bar was two deep, people who had just come to drink and people wanting refills and Madelaine and Susan too busy to help them and Mrs. Steffa no help at all.

Du Pré poured whiskey and Mrs. Steffa drew beers. All the drink orders were for whiskey ditches with either tap water or soda as mix.

The bar crowd thinned out. Some people were leaving, the money for their meals left on the tables.

"Thank you Mr. Du Pré," said Mrs. Steffa. She was short and plump and gray-blond. She meant well.

Du Pré got a big tub and he bussed the tables of dirty dishes and glasses and silverware and hauled a hundred pounds of crockery back to the kitchen, were he rinsed the dishes and put them in the huge dishwasher and put the soap in the dingus and shut the door and turned it on.

He got his drink and went back out. Madelaine was wiping the tables and Susan Klein was dragging a cart with silverware and glasses and napkins along, setting the tables back up, though the rush was all done.

Booger Tom and Bart were off in a corner eating.

Du Pré went over and he squatted down on his hunks and Booger Tom nodded, his mouth full, and Bart nodded, too.

"Good evening," said Bart. "I understand the assholes at the Messmer place don't like you."

Du Pré shrugged.

"I can have my people here in hours," said Bart. He meant the very expensive security people who worked for him. Du Pré didn't know where, exactly.

"They come," said Du Pré, "them people just wait until they are gone, you know."

"What I know of these bastards," said Bart, "I was thinking more on the lines of Madelaine and Jacqueline and Raymond and the kids. These folks play very dirty."

"It is me they want, I guess," said Du Pré. "They think I kill that Larry Messmer."

"Did you?" said Bart, grinning.

"I maybe send Madelaine, that Bassman," said Du Pré. "She got cousins, Turtle Mountain."

"Okay," said Bart, "but surely Jacqueline. Raymond. The kids."

Du Pré nodded.

Blind owls.

Bart sat back and stretched and yawned and then he had some of his lime and soda.

Booger Tom was grimly chewing with his worn old teeth.

"Bart," said Du Pré, "they are already here, so you don't got to get up, you know, make a phony call."

Bart shrugged.

"I worry about my friends," he said.

Du Pré stood up. He sipped his whiskey and nodded at Bart and Booger Tom and went back to the bar and made himself another. Mrs. Steffa was carefully pouring three-fourths of an ounce of whiskey into a glum rancher's glass.

Kelleher came in. He stood for a moment, looking around. He saw Du Pré and he waved and then he went back outside.

Du Pré waited but he didn't come back.

Finally Du Pré went to the front door and out and he looked up and down the street. There was a telephone company's truck parked under a pole and a man on top of the big tool box that took up the whole rear end was looking at some wires.

Kelleher wasn't there.

Du Pré looked at the pickups and cars parked in the lot and out on the sides of the street, but there weren't any he didn't know.

It was cold out, the wet cold of late spring.

Du Pré went back to the kitchen and he made up a thick sandwich of rare prime rib, mustard, lettuce, and sourdough and he got a can of pop and he took the sandwich out to the guy on the telephone truck.

"Thank you much," said the man, reaching in his pocket.

"Goes on Bart's bill," said Du Pré.

"Who?" said the man.

Du Pré just shrugged and he went back inside. He finished his drink.

He made another and went back to the kitchen.

Susan Klein and Madelaine were taking a break.

"Du Pré?" said Madelaine. "I think maybe I go see my cousins."

Du Pré nodded and shook his head.

Yes.

❧ CHAPTER 23 ❧

This time the music went well. Du Pré sank into old melodies, old words, long time gone. Bassman often waited so long to add bass lines Du Pré felt like he was falling with nothing under him, and then there was, when Bassman came in. Père Godin's accordion, ancient wind in the reeds, came and went like air and darkness.

The audience whooped and hollered and ranchers and their wives two-stepped. Madelaine did the clog dances, heel and toe. When Du Pré played war songs, she moved around no more than she would have dancing on a shield.

Du Pré stopped a few minutes before two. He and Bassman were all soaked in sweat. Père Godin hadn't sweated since the Second World War ended. He said he had sweated out his life at Dieppe.

"What is this Dieppe?" said Du Pré.

"Man, he come back from that, he like children," Père Godin had said.

Du Pré helped Bassman break down the sound system and he carried out the amps and soundboards. Madelaine had gone home to pack a few things, and the telephone repairman followed her.

Bassman's burlap blonde was passed out on a shelf bed in the van. She gave off sour breath in snores.

The crowd filed out and got into their trucks and cars and went off on the long drive home.

Du Pré stripped off his wet shirt in the kitchen and he put on a fresh one, heavy cotton in a close-clipped toweling. He wiped the strings on his fiddle carefully and took the tension off the horsehair in the bow.

He sipped a drink and smoked. He looked out the little window at the dark.

Me and that owl we are just as good, us, in that.

"Du Pré!" said Madelaine. She had come in the back door, quietly.

He looked up.

"We are taking a different car," she said, "that Bart got people here. That Bassman he will dick around an hour or two, then go. I am going now."

Du Pré got up.

"You got your glasses, you driving?" he said.

She kissed him.

"I am going, I will call," she said. "You stay here."

Madelaine walked away. Du Pré got up and went to the hall that led to the back door and he saw Madelaine get into a black sedan with dark windows. The car was noiseless and it pulled away.

Bassman was sitting at the bar with Susan Klein, who was counting money out in front of him.

They never charged the people who came to come in the door, but a hat got passed at the end of each set, and Du Pré's friends and neighbors were generous if the times permitted.

"They love you guys," said Susan Klein. "Twelve hundred and thirty-one dollars."

Bassman picked the money up and he swiftly made two piles of it and he stuck one roll in his pocket and took the other out the door to Père Godin, who was courting but could always be interrupted for money.

Bassman came back and he went out the back door to have some of the giant joint. It was getting cold out and air was sliding down from the Wolf Mountains.

Snow, mud, dust, Du Pré thought, three seasons we got, Montana.

Madelaine is safe she gets there.

Susan Klein was cleaning up. She had a swamper who came in early, an old man who was befuddled, and who did the floors well but didn't notice much else.

Bassman came back in and he and Du Pré shook hands.

"I go park, Madelaine's," said Bassman. "Stay the night go on tomorrow. Couple my brothers, they look out for Madelaine, Turtle Mountain, till I get there."

Du Pré nodded.

Good place, that Turtle Mountain, everybody know everybody; they don't know you you are not from there.

Now about me, the blind owl.

"That damn woman," said Bassman, nodding toward his van out front, "is worn out." He grinned. He walked out.

Du Pré waited until Susan was done with the cleaning; he helped her lock up and kill most of the lights and they left.

Du Pré got in his cruiser and he drove out to Bart's. He had a room in Bart's house, one with its own entrance and bath. The house had lights on but Bart was asleep.

Du Pré saw a strange van, a big dark one with a funny antenna on it, parked in the shadow of the machine shed.

He drew water into the big whirlpool tub and he got in and sat. His glass of whiskey and ice had a thick heavy bottom so it sat in the water like a buoy and bobbed as the jets of water stirred underneath it.

He waited till he yawned and then he went to bed and slept until first light. Three hours.

Dreamless sleep.

Bart was in the kitchen frying ham and eggs. He nodded to Du Pré and flipped a pink slab of meat over. There was plenty.

They ate without talking. Bart had a copy of a newspaper full of financial information. He read it nodding.

Du Pré cleaned up and then he went to his room and finished dressing and then went out to his cruiser. The van that had sat in the machine shed's shadow was gone. He looked around.

It was by the horse barn. A man in dark coveralls was up on the roof installing something with wires.

Booger Tom walked out of his big cabin carrying a huge blue tin cup that steamed. He waved with his free hand to Du Pré and went on toward the van.

The air was warming as the sun hit it. The day would be bright and by nightfall the line of snow on the Wolf Mountains would have moved a little closer to the peaks.

Du Pré sat in his old cruiser for a while, smoking, and then he started it and drove down to the bench road and he turned toward Benetsee's. The road was still frosty where the sun hadn't hit it. The tires either slopped or crunched.

Du Pré pulled off on a snowplow turnaround and sat awhile looking at the Wolf Mountains.

Spend my life with them there, don't feel right when I am away, the sky is lonely without them. Been other places don't feel right. My people they come down here 1886. Poor Métis got a hoe, a wagon, blankets a few, horses, lots of kids. Pick them mussels, sell the shells, button makers. Cut that sweet cedar for box makers. Live on deer and rabbits, birds, beef off a cow died sad and alone.

Benetsee he was maybe here they come.

Damn him.

Need him now.

Need him for answers, even them riddles I can't see this time. We are all afraid but nobody done nothing.

Blind fucking owl. Never see that before. Another owl eat him maybe, he is outside.

Du Pré smoked.

Sleep in the graveyard tonight, maybe even I am alive when I do that.

Talk to my people.

He started the car and he drove on and he turned in the drive that wallowed up to Benetsee's old cabin.

A pair of ravens flew up from behind it.

A magpie flashed black and white toward the creek. It dropped behind the willows.

Du Pré got his 9mm out of the glove box. He racked a shell into the chamber and he put two extra clips in his jacket pocket.

He backed down the driveway a little and then stopped and slid out in the weeds. The deer had made a path and he crouched along in twenty-foot lengths, stopping to listen.

The ravens settled on the roof of the old cabin, silent and waiting.

Du Pré got to the willows by the creek and he dove into the brush and moved forward on his hands and knees, stopping to look and listen.

He made one last dash and he could see the top of the sweat lodge. The old blankets and tarps were thrown up on top like usual.

Du Pré stood up and held his gun out. He sidestepped around the sweat lodge.

Over by the path that led to the pool where people plunged

themselves after a sweat Du Pré saw something black between the stems of the alders.

He waited looking at the house, but it was dead, and then he went to the back porch but no one had been on it.

He moved down the trail with his gun out, finger on the trigger. The 9mm was a combat pistol and had no safety.

The black was a boot sole, boot on a foot, camouflage leg, a dead man facedown near the water.

Du Pré grabbed the man's shoulder and turned him over. The face was purple with startled eyes and a thick tongue out.

Tattoo on the back of a hand.

Du Pré thought the guy was one of the hands Kelleher had brought, but there was no way of telling.

He patted the pockets, nothing but a small knife.

Du Pré walked back and he looked down into the pool.

Water weeds danced in the purling.

They pulled away from a small machine pistol, on the gravels, a simple mean-looking thing, flat black so the light would not jump off it into an enemy's eyes.

❧ CHAPTER 24 ❧

I dunno what you mean," said Kelleher, "I never saw the guy before, really."

His face was as bland as vanilla pudding.

"Mr. Kelleher," said Benny Klein, "thanks so much for dropping by. You've helped immeasurably."

Kelleher walked out.

"That prick is lying," said Benny, "but I sure as shit can't prove it."

The body of the man with the purple face was on its way to Billings for autopsy.

Du Pré was sitting on the counter, cleaning his nails with a pen knife.

"Harvey will have pictures," said Benny. "Whoever the asshole is I expect he has been photographed and fingerprinted at the taxpayer's expense a few times."

"Who kill him?" said Du Pré. "This guy is there maybe waiting."

Benny looked at him.

"Goddamn it, Du Pré," said Benny, "I couldn't track a streak of shit across a blackboard. When we were out baggin' up the late Mr. John Doe *you* were off fartin' around in the bushes. Don't give me this crap."

Du Pré nodded.

Guy is getting around the back there, hide near the sweat and there is this guy there, moccasins, he is waiting with a garrote. Asshole we find don't have time, hide. He is dead when he gets there. Don't see nothing, either.

Remember the Army, you are garroting a sentry, you loop the wire around the neck, turn, lift the guy on your back and whirl around. He can't do nothing. Sergeant say, cut a guy's throat it is noisy, do it this way.

Russians come, over that German border, me, I am not strangling no sentries, I am maybe staying down in the foxhole, shoot once in a while, come up every hour or so, see how things are going.

"Maybe he piss Kelleher off, he have him killed," said Du Pré.

"Maybe somebody pitched him out of a plane," said Benny.

The telephone rang and the dispatcher waved at Benny.

"Oh, darn you," said Benny, handing the phone to Du Pré.

"He doesn't like me," said Harvey.

"Benny, him don't like dead bodies," said Du Pré. "He is sheriff it is ver' brave since he is a kind man. This guy you know maybe?"

"Oh," said Harvey, "he is an old friend. We have known of each other for years and years. Richard Lee Masters, though his best friends all called him Bongo. One of his best friends was the late Larry Messmer. They used to murder and extort together, burn down something here and there, run whores, move large amounts of drugs and stolen cars and motorcycles. Bongo was a sort of handyman, not very bright but quite trustworthy. He got arrested a lot but only did seven on a bank robbery charge. He was supposed to drive the getaway car, but, a sad tale, he had never driven anything but automatics so he was still trying to find first gear when the fuzz arrived. His accomplices had beat feet by then, hijacking a car, and leaving poor Bongo, who would not snitch on them. He was at least bright enough to know that would lead to his early death."

"Army?" said Du Pré.

"High point of Bongo's career," said Harvey. "He actually made it through basic and advanced infantry training before succumbing to an urge to steal a car. The Army was merciful, and left him in the stockade for six months before kicking him out. Dishonorable discharge, of course."

"So why is he there, Benetsee's?" said Du Pré.

"To kill you, of course," said Harvey.

"Why they kill me anyway?" said Du Pré.

"We did this," said Harvey. "They think you killed Messmer."

"I don't, though," said Du Pré.

"They don't care," said Harvey, "somebody did. Since it was no one they know, they figure it has to be you. These are not terribly bright guys, Du Pré. They're sort of like the Nixon Administration, you know, a lot of dumb guys trying to be smart. We wouldn't bother with them, but you know how it is."

"Me, I don't know how it is," said Du Pré.

"I can't talk about it," said Harvey.

"You Blackfeet prick," said Du Pré, "you don't be saying to me, Du Pré, do me this favor."

"Shit," said Harvey, "I'll be there soon. Give my best to Madelaine."

Du Pré handed the phone back to Benny.

"Him come," said Du Pré, "I break his fucking jaw."

"Du Pré," said Benny, "that's assault. Our silly legislature says so. Cain't even bust a man's jaw you got reason anymore. The social workers will smother you 'fore you ever get to court anyway."

"Bongo," said Du Pré, "Is what they call that guy."

"Bongo?" said Benny.

Du Pré nodded. He went out to his old cruiser and he got in and drove back out to Benetsee's. The lines through the grass where the ambulance had gone were deep.

The ground around the sweat lodge was torn up from cop feet and the ambulance guys and the coroner and about thirty curious citizens.

I got moccasin tracks, I got two beads, Du Pré thought, and this guy he likes me some and so far he is better than they are.

Du Pré looked up at the butte.

He started walking. The trail was clear for two miles and then flakes of the mountain began to stick out and then it got steep when he went to the knee of the mountain that held the butte against the Wolfs. The last ten feet were straight up and long ago someone had hacked footholds and handholds in the limestone.

Du Pré got up top and he sat for a while till his breath came back. Then he stood up and started walking around the edge of the butte, and each time he passed the way up he went in four feet.

There were dozens of little cairns of rock the mountains did not make, and blackened fire rings and even half a round of stones, the sort used to hold down the skirts of teepees.

Sioux been here, Blackfeet been here, Shoshone been here long time gone, Crow been here too.

Got no initials and they don't leave names.

Come here, maybe slash their arms, bleed, make the visions come quicker. Don't eat, don't drink, don't move. But you got to piss and you got to shit.

There was a tiny stand of warped and twisted pines in a cleft on a flat place near the center of the butte.

Goddamn me I should have damn well come up here that first time.

Du Pré saw the print of a small black bear in yellow mud, hard now after days with no rain.

Son of a bitch come here, eat everything.

Du Pré dropped to his hunks and he stared and let the ground float up to him and sit there. Tracks of mice in the dust by the rock. Owl's wings touch there and there.

Man squat there out of sight, man goes someplace out of sight it is a habit we got.

Hold on to that rock there lean back so you don't hit your pants on the ground.

Du Pré saw a bright black eye shining in a tiny cleft in the rock. A pika edged its head out toward the light.

Du Pré sat still.

The pika came out farther and then it squeaked and disappeared.

Du Pré took his knife out and he opened the long blade. He carefully began to lift small stones, flat ones spalled from the rocks on either side.

A black beetle sat sullen in the light.

Spider. Little one.

Du Pré carefully picked up each rock and tossed it over his shoulder.

A quill gone orange in time.

Goddamn me I should have not been so lazy. Come up here, time gone. Him got them moccasins, he was here.

Something white. Paper, what the bear didn't eat. A small shred.

Du Pré moved forward a foot and he lifted another rock slowly.

A velvet ant, the wingless wasp with the noise box in its abdomen, shrilled feebly.

Don't see one of them, years and years.

Du Pré saw a small round black turd. He opened a little plastic envelope and worried the turd into it with the knife point. He shut the envelope and put it in his pocket.

He lifted up another rock. A flake of jasper under it, maybe a small scraper, maybe not.

He lifted all the flakes and found nothing but a few bugs.

He stood up.

Okay.

What's next?

✤ CHAPTER 25 ✤

M y goodness, Gabriel," said Miss Porterfield, "I wondered so over the years when exactly you would want to look at the materials. Why, you know that your great-great-great-grandfathers fought the English in 1870 and . . . well, your people surely are fascinating."

Du Pré nodded.

Past, it is blurry with people my blood come from. Me, I am related to all of Manitoba and Saskatchewan and half of Alberta. Thing about mongrels, they survive.

"These are only copies," said Miss Porterfield. "Poor carbon copies at that. But Father Tannay was so meticulous and kind. He was working on a history of the Métis, but . . . there was some trouble or other and his superiors directed him to stop. He died shortly after. Why, I had to go all the way to Montréal and beg to get these. I said, well, it was so long ago, who could it hurt? Poor Father Tannay, he was in some trouble for heresy, too, and . . . well, he liked . . . small boys."

Du Pré nodded. Got a Jesuit with some gaskets gone, send him the Métis, most of us got gone gaskets, too.

"Have you met Mr. Jacquot yet, the nice young man who is staying out at the Martins?" said Miss Porterfield. "He's an historian. He tells me he's fascinated by the Métis. He says he's proposing to do his doctoral dissertation on the rebellions and the dispersions."

Meaning they run our ass all over the place, steal the Métis lands, some of us run down here, run to Red River country, North Dakota, go back, come back, mostly live, teepees, by the dumps on the edge of the little towns. Dumps are gone because the little towns are gone, the Métis are gone, the teepees, few of us move into the towns. Most of us look white, become white, we are gone.

Not my Papa Catfoot. He say, damn, we are the people, you know, we are the ones guide that Lewis and Clark, we are the Mountain Men, we are the Indian scouts, we got our music we got our language we got our stories. We don't buy us funny suits, sell them cars. We are Métis.

Catfoot he play that proud music.

Old man tell me, Catfoot say, Métis are here before Champlain. Champlain he come, silly ostrich feathers, some damn thing, his hat, he is ass end of nowhere up the Saint Lawrence River, see some Indians, over there, the shore. Champlain he row over, got a Métis interpreter. Ask them how it is going for them today, Champlain say to the interpreter. Interpreter speak, them Indians. Priests, they have it better, says one Indian, in French. Champlain go on, looking for Indians don't speak that French, so he can discover them.

Long time gone.

Ain't them Jesuits go on before Champlain, teach Indians that French. First Jesuit, he is with Champlain, looking for Indians don't speak that French so he can discover them, save their souls.

Us Métis, have a lot of babies, do hard work, rest of you do what you maybe want.

"Gabriel!" said Miss Porterfield, her voice sharp and a little angry.

"Uh," said Du Pré.

"You're daydreaming. You always did that in school, too. I

would look out at the class and all of them would be paying attention to the lesson and you would be daydreaming."

Du Pré nodded. Beats the shit out of watching Dick and Jane run.

"I asked if you had met Mr. Jacquot," said Miss Porterfield.

"Yah," said Du Pré. "Him come to the bar, Toussaint, once. College boy playing cowboy, we get them."

"He's a fine young man," said Miss Porterfield. Her eyes were red and her hands trembled a little. She set down the folder with the thin sheaf of papers in it. She held her right hand with her left. She looked toward the bar, which was open but empty.

"Me," said Du Pré, "I buy you a brandy, maybe two."

"It's too *early*," said Miss Porterfield.

"Bar is open it is not too early," said Du Pré. He led her in and they got up on stools.

Velma came out of the back. She looked at Miss Porterfield and then Du Pré and then she shrugged. She got a glass and heated it and put a big slug of brandy in it and slid it over and then she made a ditch for Du Pré. She picked up the twenty that Du Pré had laid on the bar top and made change and then she shrugged again and went in the back.

Miss Porterfield drank her brandy in a long swallow and then she put a napkin to her lips and belched very softly. She just sat and looked at the mirror behind the bar for a few minutes. Then she got off the stool.

"I must visit the necessary," she said, going off toward the bathrooms. Her walk was steady now.

Velma came back out.

"She's killin' herself," said Velma. "You know she did this for years, but lately she's drinkin' more and more. Oh, she's so sweet, but, Jesus, Du Pré, she can't do this, her liver'll blow up."

Du Pré nodded.

"Maybe she want that," he said, "you know, she don't teach, she is not happy. What you want her to do, get that religion?"

Velma looked sad a moment.

"I want to be her friend, but I don't know how," she said.

Du Pré nodded.

"I maybe ask that Bart come talk to her," he said.

"Jesus," said Velma. "He was a terror. Been dry a while now?"

Du Pré nodded.

"Okay," said Velma, "I feel better now. Didn't know what to do. You sure he'll talk to her?"

Du Pré nodded.

Velma made up another brandy and another ditch and she left them and didn't take Du Pré's money. She went on toward the back.

Miss Porterfield came back from the bathroom. She had washed her face in cold water and drops clung to her gray-white hair. She had cleaned her glasses. She stood upright.

She slid up on the stool.

"Velma's very liberal today," she said. "I thought I should have to fight for this one."

Du Pré looked at the papers in the folder. Each family tale told by an old woman took about a page and a half of double-spaced script, badly smudged, some letters just solid black blocks.

"Terrible reading," said Miss Porterfield. "These old women were so devout, and they felt their sorrows came from God and so they were good. But you can read between the lines. The old people and the babies dying of cold and hunger. The soldiers after them, American soldiers trying to drive them back across the border where the Canadians waited, angry for the Red River Re-bellions. Their lands gone, their stock, crops, homes."

Du Pré nodded.

Lots of songs about that.

"This Messmer, the old one, that Albert," said Du Pré, "him have an Indian wife, he is first here."

"Yes," said Miss Porterfield, "her name was Genevette, some corruption of Genevieve, I suppose. She was Assiniboine, I think."

Assiniboines very beautiful women, plenty Métis, them Assiniboines.

Genevette.

"Genevette," said Du Pré.

"Odd name," said Miss Porterfield.

Genevette.

Du Pré watched the blue smoke from his cigarette curl up.

White man tell her, you must go, here is some food, a sled, you pull your babies through the snow. My white wife she is coming and you better not be here.

Genevette she pull her babies through the snow, her hands freeze to the leather straps she pulls with, she got no snowshoes, her feet they freeze, but she walks and walks while her babies sleep warm in furs on that sled, finds some Métis camped many miles along. They take her in, but her hands and feet turn black and she dies.

Genevette's ghost, you see her north of here sometime, in the snow storm, just at twilight or at dawn, pulling her sled and babies through the snow.

Métis they always carry extra blankets, buffalo robes, clothes, they take them along, one bundle, they say for Genevette, she might come. Like they always have an extra plate for Jesus, might come in hungry any time. Even they are starving, little piece of something on that plate.

Du Pré stubbed out his cigarette, the music from the Song of Genevette in his head. Pret' new song, new words, old melody. Melodies, they are ver' old, words, newer. Words are easy.

There are always new stories.

144

Miss Porterfield got down and she said good-bye and she went out the front door, home to sleep awhile.

Du Pré took the folder and his drink and went to a table and began to read.

✤ CHAPTER 26 ✤

Harvey and a younger agent stood in the Toussaint Saloon, stretching muscles cramped first on the long flight and then the longer drive from Billings to Toussaint.

Du Pré looked at the younger agent's feet.

Hiking boots, lightweight ones.

"Him don't got them wingtips," said Du Pré, "you are sure this is an FBI agent? Harvey, eh?"

"Knock him on his ass, Ripper," said Harvey, looking at the younger agent.

"Now," said Ripper, "it's a fair question. I don't own a pair of wingtips. Probably why promotions are so damn slow. Glad to meet you, Du Pré."

He held out his hand and Du Pré shook it.

"The Ripster here did a few years undercover," said Harvey. "Matter of fact, went under and tried to get in with Messmer's bunch. Didn't work."

"Oh," said Du Pré.

"Messmer's bunch requires sincere applicants," said Harvey. "They blindfold you and take you off someplace, after stripping you carefully and giving you a jumpsuit, so there isn't a homing beacon in your shoe heel, and when the blindfold comes off they give you a gun and you shoot some screaming woman just got to her big scene in a snuff film. You don't shoot, they say, well, you flunk, and on goes the blindfold and back you go and they tell you to go away."

"A crude but effective filter," said Ripper. "Since I can't commit any illegal acts and I draw the line at murder in my personal life, too. Yup, failed that one miserably."

"What happened the woman?" said Du Pré.

"Somebody else shot her," said Ripper. "We know this because the snuff film surfaced. These are not nice people."

"You see this film?" said Du Pré.

Ripper nodded and he looked at the floor.

"I puked for an hour after," he said. "I mean to get these bastards."

"Me, too," said Harvey. "Matter of fact, we thought we'd come here and maybe sweat Kelleher a little, since the asshole knows us both."

Ripper looked angry.

"He was there," he said. "They all had on ski masks, of course, but that fat fuck was the one who waddled over and offered me the gun. Ain't nobody walks like him but him."

"Duck test," said Harvey. "He passed it."

"Madelaine she is in North Dakota," said Du Pré.

"Good," said Harvey. "What about Raymond and Jacqueline and the kids."

"Bart got some people here," said Du Pré.

Harvey nodded.

"The late Bongo was waiting to kill you," said Harvey. "I expect that Kelleher thinks you did it."

Du Pré shook his head.

Harvey looked at him for a long moment.

"What have you got for me?" said Harvey.

"A turd," said Du Pré.

"Perfect," said Ripper. "It's your day, Harv."

Du Pré grinned at the young agent. He was in his late twenties, with thick brown hair left long, lightly built but wiry. His intelligent brown eyes looked through thick granny glasses. He was not afraid of Harvey.

Du Pré fished the little plastic envelope out and handed it to Harvey, who glanced at it and offered it to Ripper.

"Fine specimen," said Ripper. "Now what do we want to know about it?"

"What the guy ate," said Du Pré.

"Okay," said Ripper, "I saw a FedEx box on the edge of town. Excuse me, I got to go. They have fucking Federal Express here? They shove it up a coyote and set his tail on fire? They got electricity and everything, I am told." He went out still reciting modern wonders found in Toussaint, Montana.

"Good kid," said Harvey, "recruited him myself. Son of the next-door neighbor. Brave little son of a bitch. After college, he wanted a little adventure, so he flew to South America and then he jumped out of an airplane at the headwaters of the Amazon, with a fucking kayak, and showed up six months later in Brasilia. Wouldn't comment on the trip other'n it was a lot more fun than he expected, almost more than he could stand."

"You got other guys here?" said Du Pré.

"A couple," said Harvey, "sort of blending in around, you know. I told them look, no wingtips, guys."

Du Pré nodded.

"Well," said Harvey, "want to maybe drive us out, to that asshole Kelleher? They won't scatter as fast they see that old piece of shit you drive. We got the usual guvverment sedan, guvverment tan. Bald front tires, too."

"Sure," said Du Pré.

They went out and waited for Ripper to come back from the FedEx box.

He grinned.

"He's driving us?" said the young agent. "How nice."

"You haven't ridden with him," said Harvey.

"I hope he drives fast," said Ripper, "since all the way up here my Great-Auntie Harvey was going fifty-five. Billings is a long damn way from here at fifty-five."

"The front end's out of alignment," said Harvey.

"Yes, Auntie," said Ripper.

Du Pré laughed.

They got in his old cruiser and Du Pré started it and drove off and he turned after a while and headed up to the bench road and then the Messmer place.

Three hands were chasing the horses around the big pasture, and not much else. The horses wouldn't go through the gate of the round corral, because one of the hands had left a shirt on the gate and the cloth flapped in the wind.

Du Pré parked right by the old ranch house and got out and he went to the door and he was about to hit it when it opened and Kelleher came out, face broad and smiling.

"Mr. Du Pré!" he said. "Good to see you. Say, I had a couple of questions about the . . ."

He looked over and he started and his eyes got scared for just a moment.

"Kelleher, you fat fuck," said Ripper. "Say, that girl I wouldn't shoot, somebody did, Kelleher. I hope it was you, you cocksucker, so I can bust you for it, then watch you die. Nice lethal injection."

"Who is this man, Mr. Du Pré?" said Kelleher.

Du Pré shrugged.

"I . . . you leave now," said Kelleher. "Quit trespassing. Get out."

He was getting red and angry and scared.

"You got questions about horses?" said Du Pré.

"Not important," said Kelleher. "Go now. I will call the Sheriff. I will do that right now." He turned to go inside.

"We're leaving, you fat fuck," said Ripper, "but we'll be baaaaaaack."

He got back in the car.

Du Pré grabbed Kelleher's shoulder and he turned him around. He stared into Kelleher's piggy eyes until the man's gaze broke.

"This is all over," said Du Pré, "I will still be here, where you maybe be, eh, Kelleher? That Bongo guy is yours. I get the pictures from them FBI, I come back, a warrant, deputies."

"Get out of here!" Kelleher screamed.

Du Pré let go. He walked back to the car.

He got in.

"He doesn't like us," said Ripper.

"Ripper," said Harvey, "if I wasn't completely deaf I would have to file a report on you, one stating that you broke about six rules there, and you know how we at the FBI are about rules."

"Eight," said Ripper. "I broke eight rules, Harvey. But since you are deaf, well, it hardly matters because like any devoted public servant I lie with a clear conscience, because if I had a conscience which was nice and murky, I would go get a real job."

"Hopeless," said Harvey.

Du Pré turned around and drove out. The hands were still trying to drive the horses in the corral.

"Gosh," said Harvey, "it sure has been good to see you, Du Pré."

"You are going?" said Du Pré.

"Yup," said Harvey.

"We just came to make Kelleher's day," said Ripper. "Got to drive all the way back to Billings at fifty-five."

"Bitch bitch bitch," said Harvey.

150

"What you come for anyway?" said Du Pré.

"These guys aren't very smart, really," said Ripper, "but they got a few rules they don't break. Maybe they get upset, they get careless."

"Who you got here anyway?" said Du Pré.

Harvey looked at him a long time. Then he shook his head.

✤ CHAPTER 27 ✤

The air turned soft. The flowers rioted on the foothills and along the watercourses and clover bloomed. It was the few days between winter and the dusty summer when the earth held water for a moment.

People opened the windows of their houses and let air wash through. They looked at the beds of iris and the camas lilies, up and brilliant and gone in a week.

Du Pré woke up. Someone was tapping on the door that led outside.

He had slept late, which he rarely did.

"Jesus," said Booger Tom, "thought you'd died. Christ, man, it is after nine o'clock."

Du Pré yawned.

Booger Tom was carrying his huge blue enamel cup. Du Pré could smell coffee and whiskey. The old man sat on the stoop.

"I'll just wait here till you're done with your manicure," said Booger Tom.

Du Pré shut the door. He got dressed and he went to the kitchen. Bart was there, cooking breakfast.

"I'll go see Miss Porterfield," said Bart, "but you know it never does any good. To just go talk to someone."

"It will make that Velma feel better," said Du Pré.

Du Pré cracked three raw eggs in a glass and he dashed Tabasco on them and then he drank them down. He poured a big cup of coffee in a red tin cup and he carried it back through his room, yawning. He went out the door and sat down beside Booger Tom.

"They done broke a couple horse's legs out to Messmer's," said Booger Tom. "Had to shoot 'em. It was all stupidity done it. I was thinkin' if you could get a warrant on them horses bein' abused we could take 'em."

"Don't got no warrants," said Du Pré. "And that Benny . . . I don't think he would do that."

"They's ruinin' good stock," said Booger Tom.

Du Pré drank his coffee.

"What they are doing out there it is not the horses anyway," said Du Pré, "it is something else."

"They turn them horses out in that pasture by that lake they made," said Booger Tom. "Some of them'll get stuck in the mud, too. Talking about something else that makes no sense."

Du Pré shrugged.

"Feller could get in there and look around," said Booger Tom.

"They got them cameras, alarms," said Du Pré.

Motion detectors. Floodlights.

Crow have them, we don't steal so many of their horses.

"That damn pond is so shallow," said Booger Tom, "and when the melt stops it ain't gonna be anything but some tussock grass and bare ground."

Du Pré nodded.

"You know that young feller, Jerry, stayin' over to Martins?" said Booger Tom, "sent me a nice letter sayin' how he like to interview me for some book he's doin'. I expect I'll let him."

Du Pré drank coffee.

Him one of Harvey's guys, no wingtips. Special select FBIs.

"I think he's something else," said Booger Tom. "Why a bright young feller'd like to talk to me don't make any sense."

Du Pré snorted.

153

"Why," said Booger Tom, "there he is now."

A new SUV, dark blue, with chrome racks and mag wheels, was coming up the driveway. The driver slowed when he got to the big turn yard and he drove right up to Du Pré and Booger Tom, stopping slowly.

Jerry Jacquot got out, a big smile on his face. He had a little flat briefcase. He walked over to Du Pré and Booger Tom and stood for a moment.

"Mornin'," said Jacquot, "Mr. Du Pré and Mr. Booger Tom."

"We was just settin' here bein' colorful," said Booger Tom, "but we're off at ten."

Du Pré stood up.

"Someplace we can talk?" said Jacquot. "I need a table top to set up my computer here."

"Computer," said Booger Tom.

"Yup," said Jacquot. "Child of the eighties. Times I grew up in."

"Christ," said Booger Tom, getting up, "I expect my cabin'll do."

"Du Pré," said Bart, "you got a call."

Du Pré went inside to the kitchen and picked up the telephone.

"It's Agent Ripper," said Ripper, "and a jolly good morning. That specimen you sent us. Got a partial analysis. Better one takes longer. Usual stuff. Except for one thing. Raspberry seeds."

Du Pré waited.

"They were unusual," said Ripper, "because they hadn't been cooked. Jam gets cooked. Raspberry muffins get cooked. These were raw seeds. Put in the ground, little water, sheep shit, they'd sprout, make more raspberries."

"Yah," said Du Pré.

"Well," said Ripper, "that's it. Whoever left that had a little money. Raspberries are about four bucks for a half pint this time of year."

154

"Okay," said Du Pré, "now maybe you tell me what the fuck you and that Harvey were maybe doing here?"

"Stirring the shit," said Ripper. "We do that when we are pissed off. Harvey's been after this bunch for years."

"You are lying to me," said Du Pré.

"Sure am," said Ripper. "FBI policy."

"Is that Harvey there?" said Du Pré.

"That ugly Blackfeet bastard," said Ripper, "who makes my life as miserable as he can? The prick? Yeah, he's here."

"I talk to him," said Du Pré.

"I will check that for you," said Ripper. He put his hand over the mouthpiece of the telephone.

"He isn't here," said Ripper. "Just stepped out of the office."

"Tell him I call his wife, tell her he plays around," said Du Pré.

Ripper put his hand back over the mouthpiece.

"You want me dead?" said Harvey.

"This kid Jacquot he is one of yours?" said Du Pré.

"No comment," said Harvey.

"Bullshit your no comment," said Du Pré.

"Easy, Du Pré," said Harvey, "you know how it is."

Du Pré hung up.

He poured some more coffee and went out to his old cruiser and checked the trunk.

The MP-40 Catfoot had brought back from the big war was there, in the old stained bow case. Four extra magazines. The original machine pistol. Heavy. 9mm. Fast-fire. Some people called it the Schmeisser.

Du Pré put the bow case on the front seat and he got in and started the cruiser and he drove down the road and turned off toward Benetsee's cabin. It was a few miles before the rutted track through the tall grass appeared just beyond the huge puddle at the roadside.

155

Du Pré drove up near to the cabin and he parked where he always did.

He opened the door and looked around.

Nobody had been there since the last time Du Pré had parked here.

He slid the MP-40 out of the case and he unfolded the stock and checked the magazine and armed the gun, pulling the slide. He put the spare magazines in his hip pocket. He walked around behind the cabin.

A raven flew up from the creekside. It hung in the air and then slowly flew off.

Du Pré walked carefully around the yard. The sweat lodge was cold and the firepit still held the wood that the man who had killed Bongo had cut. The man on the butte.

Du Pré sat on the stump. He bent his head and he breathed deep.

My old friend I need you. You got to come now, got to speak. I can't see, me, this.

Old bastard.

Du Pré went to the firepit. The wood was stacked tight and it was dry except for the bottom layer, against the wet ashes.

Du Pré put the machine pistol down. He put the rocks for the sweat on top of the woodpile. He went to the cruiser and he got some paper and lighter fluid. He started the fire and then he carefully stuck split sticks into the flames.

The fire roared and the rick collapsed and the stones lay heating on a thick bed of red coals.

When they were dusty white Du Pré carried them to the lodge and piled them in the steam pit. He stripped and he got in and he flipped down the door.

My machine pistol it is out there, damn Benetsee better see that no one comes, uses it.

Du Pré poured water on the hot rocks. The steam billowed, hissing.

Du Pré began to chant, prayer chant, help me chant.

He poured water.

Heat.

✤ CHAPTER 28 ✤

S orry I took so long to get back to you," said the vet. "I had to send tissue samples off to a lab in Minneapolis."

Du Pré waited. His sinuses had dried up when he sweated and if he spoke he sneezed shortly thereafter.

"The coyote died of 'complex poisoning' is what the lab says, and then they go on to say the most likely toxins were agricultural chemicals mixed with petrochemicals. The coyote got into some bad water. Probably drank from a pool where fertilizers and petroleum met. There weren't any signs of 1080 or heavy metals."

"Does this happen much?" asked Du Pré.

"I don't know," said the vet. "Very few people are upset when they see a dying coyote around here. You're the first one who ever bothered to bring one in."

"Thank you," said Du Pré. He sneezed and he sneezed.

"Only other thing I noticed was it had a burn on the left front foot. Just reddened, the skin hadn't even bubbled up when the coyote died. But it was fairly deep. It was also a cold burn, the fur wasn't singed at all."

"Cold burn?" said Du Pré.

"You ever have a wart frozen off?" said the vet. "That's a cold burn. Extreme heat or extreme cold kills the cells, blows them apart, and then new skin comes up."

"Yah," said Du Pré.

The vet hung up.

Du Pré went on to the deck at the back of Bart's house and he sat on the railing and he looked up at the Wolf Mountains.

Cold-burned coyotes, bastards with machine pistols waiting for me, whole damn country went crazy on me.

Du Pré saw a pair of men moving in the landscape, trotting over a grassy knoll and then dropping down into the coulee.

"Old son of a bitch!" said Du Pré.

Benetsee and Pelon.

Du Pré rolled a cigarette and lit it while he waited.

Old fart do that, fuck with me, old bastard. Flash across the hills, disappear.

Benetsee and Pelon appeared again, their shuffling trot the ground-eating movement of peoples here before the horse.

Du Pré waited and they came through the side gate and then they just walked slowly to him.

That old man hold the earth up here, maybe all of it, I don't know, Du Pré thought.

He went inside and he got some wine from the room Bart had stocked with priceless bottles for his guests and Du Pré grabbed one, not even bothering to read the label until he had prised the cork out.

Lynch-Bages.

Du Pré got a pair of plastic glasses and he went back out on the deck and he poured some wine for them.

Benetsee drank his down in one swallow and held the glass out.

Pelon sipped his. He was sweating. The old man was dry.

"Pret' good, this," said Benetsee.

Du Pré fetched another couple of bottles. There was screw-top wine in a jug in the trunk of his car, but Bart's stock was handier.

"Old man," said Du Pré, "I maybe need you, help me."

"Good," said Benetsee. "Lot of years you did not think that."
Du Pré sighed.

Lot of years I think he is just some old drunk. Catfoot knows better, but I am young and think my father is a fool, too.

"You maybe drive us, my house," said Benetsee. He picked up the two unopened bottles of wine. Du Pré went in the house and he got a big rib roast from the freezer and a loaf of the good bread that Madelaine had baked; there were many in the freezer, too, and when they were thawed they almost tasted fresh.

Benetsee and Pelon were already in the back seat of the old cruiser when Du Pré came out with his packages.

He got in and started the car and turned and drove down the long drive to the county road.

Benetsee and Pelon slept.

He is making me know he will not always be here, Du Pré thought, making me see as much as I can.

What is this? My Madelaine is away, frightened, my daughter and her children guarded night and day.

Me, I know who wants me dead, I did not do what they think I did.

How they hear about me?

Benetsee's old cabin crouched like a dead gray bird on the little hump of earth, good drainage when it rained. The doors and windows were closed, a magpie sat on the rooftree and then it flew away, silently.

Benetsee wheezed and coughed and he scratched himself and farted when Du Pré stopped the car. The old man looked around and then he opened his door and got out. He carried the two expensive bottles of wine inside.

Pelon went around to the back.

Du Pré carried in the bread and meat.

An axe thudded into wood.

The cabin was cold and smelled musty.

Mice scampered for cover.

Benetsee had taken off one of his running shoes and he had peeled the lead foil away from the neck of the bottle of Lynch-Bages and he turned the bottle upside down and beat on it with the soft rubber shoe.

The cork inched out.

When it got out halfway Benetsee stuck it in his mouth and bit and twisted. The cork came free.

The old man tipped up the bottle and drank it all without stopping.

He smacked his lips.

"That Bart," he said, "he is a good man."

Du Pré laughed.

Lynch-Bages. Wonder how much a bottle that is. Bart tell me some, them wines, are five hundred dollars a bottle.

"We come back, you get into trouble," said Benetsee. "Me, I think you maybe do what I do this time."

Du Pré nodded and he waited.

Do what?

"Don't do nothing," said Benetsee.

Okay.

"That old woman, the teacher," said Benetsee, "we go see her tonight."

Du Pré nodded.

Pelon came in with an armload of wood. He stacked the stove and he dribbled lighter fluid on the wood and he touched it off and the stove was roaring and giving off heat in minutes.

Benetsee sat back on the old broken chair he was in.

He closed his eyes.

161

Warmth bloomed in the room.

Du Pré saw flames out in back, too. Pelon had touched off the rick in the pit where the stones were heated for a sweat.

"I just sweat," said Du Pré.

Benetsee nodded.

Pelon picked up the white-paper–wrapped rib roast and he went out.

"Don't sweat this time," said Benetsee. "Cook meat."

Frozen fifteen-pound chunk, take a long time, Du Pré thought.

"Don't take that long," said Benetsee. "Him, he know magic."

Du Pré laughed and he rolled himself a cigarette. Benetsee looked at him. Du Pré lit the smoke and handed it over.

No use, ask questions, he tell me when he wants to, what he wants to.

"That Harvey Weasel Fat is a fool," said Benetsee.

Du Pré nodded.

Okay.

"That woman shot in the head, some years," said Benetsee.

Du Pré looked at him.

Janet Messmer.

Killed and dumped behind a gravel pile, the county road works.

"You got your fiddle?" said Benetsee.

Du Pré nodded. He got up and went out to the cruiser and opened the trunk and took out the old stained rawhide case. He carried it in. He opened it and took the bow out and tightened the hair and then he jabbed at a few notes.

Pret' damn close.

Du Pré noddled around some parts of old songs, one melody going into another.

A smell of burning fat wafted in the window.

Du Pré closed his eyes.

He wandered among the songs, thousands of them that he knew.

Long time gone.

He found the one he half remembered.

A young man's family is killed by the Sioux.

He goes after them.

I die maybe, the song says, but I go, I go for you.

There are many Sioux and just the one young man.

The young man surprises the Sioux one by one.

The Sioux set a trap for him.

The young man sings a song.

Then it is the night.

❖ CHAPTER 29 ❖

Miss Porterfield's little house was a mail-order bungalow, the kind brought in on railroad flatcars and put up on the foundation in three days. It was white, and had three small bedrooms, kitchen, living room, bath, and a parlor to the right of the front door big enough for six people to sit in and watch a coffin, discuss a daughter's hand in marriage, or have tea for no good reason at all.

Benetsee had slipped out of the back seat of Du Pré's car and gone up the crazy broken walk to the front door, up two steps from the ground. He waited there until Du Pré came along. Pelon sat in the car, head down, sleeping.

When Du Pré got up to him, Benetsee opened the front door and went in. Du Pré followed.

The air was heavy with brandy, potpourri, wax, and sorrow.

Miss Porterfield had passed out in her overstuffed chair, among the stacks of books and papers that rose from the floor and slumped together, or had collapsed into a welter of paper and buckram and old mail opened and tossed aside.

Miss Porterfield snored. A silver thread of spit hung down from the lowest corner of her mouth. Her clothes were rumpled around her, the collar of her blouse was smudged with makeup.

Benetsee bent over and he looked at her.

Miss Porterfield's eyes opened and she looked a long time at the old man's face in front of her.

"You . . . " she said finally. She shook herself and yawned, gold gleamed in the back of her mouth.

She sat forward and she put her head in her hands.

"I'm so tired," she said.

Benetsee patted her cheek.

He reached down to the floor and picked up a half-full bottle of brandy. He found the glass on the little table beside her, and put some brandy in it, and he held it in front of her nose.

Miss Porterfield took the glass in both hands and she drank the brandy down. She coughed. She sat back with her eyes closed.

"I was dreaming," she said.

Du Pré looked off into the little parlor.

Photographs in oval frames. A Sioux lance and shield. A pair of big bull horns, old, rat-gnawed. A gunbelt with an ancient nickel-plated Colt revolver in it. Some angora chaps, moth-eaten.

Beadwork. Wristlets and chokers and stomachers and aprons and headbands and even a long cape of beads, big blue trade beads.

The little pickup truck she drove was sitting out in front, on a tiny patch of bricks set in the grass.

Du Pré sighed.

Miss Porterfield got up. She lifted her glasses up and looked through the smudged lenses. She tried cleaning them on a dirty napkin that sat on a plate with some dried food stuck to it. She held the glasses up. The smudges were smears.

"I'm sorry," she said, meekly.

Benetsee poured her some more brandy. He held it out and she drank it down.

"Du Pré," said Benetsee, "you get that Bart to come here now."

Du Pré nodded. He walked toward the kitchen and he found the phone on the wall just inside the doorway.

Bart answered on the first ring.

Du Pré talked a moment, Bart said he would be right there, and they hung up.

When he went back, Miss Porterfield was laughing, her color had returned, and she was tucking her blouse into her long skirt and pushing stray strands of gray-white hair back from her eyes.

"So good of you to come," she said. "I have waited here so very long."

Du Pré looked at her and he started. She was animated and smiling, and facing Benetsee, but her eyes were on someone else who wasn't there.

Du Pré bent over and he held his lips close to Benetsee's ear.

"She is crazy?" he said.

"Dying," said Benetsee. "She is dying. But she got something to tell you, me, maybe."

"I am forgetting myself," said Miss Porterfield. "Do come into the parlor and sit down."

Du Pré stepped back to let her pass. She found the switch on an old yellowed silk lamp, the cloth peeling away from the plaster form, the tassels mostly nubs.

"So very good of you to come," said Miss Porterfield, as she fiddled with the switch.

Benetsee went in, he flicked the light switch and a bulb overhead came on, stark and white and new.

"So how is Myron? And the children?" said Miss Porterfield.

She nodded at an answer only she could hear.

"How nice," she said.

Du Pré waited.

Benetsee pointed at a photograph, a small oval of black-and-white with a jagged stripe of torn paper running across it where it had been ripped in half. The photograph was in a cheap plastic box frame, the kind sold in drugstores.

"Well," said Miss Porterfield, looking down at her hands in her lap, she had sat on a dainty little ice-cream chair, "I have told you so very many times that that day she just came by here for a while, she was quite upset, you know, she wanted to know all about poor Genevette and Albert Messmer."

Miss Porterfield nodded.

She was listening to a complicated question.

"It was about four in the afternoon," she said. She looked up, she cocked her head a little. "When she came. I had the collections, of course, and the copies of the stories. She said that she really had to know. I brought her a little drink and we held each other. It was the torn picture that seemed to hurt her so. She cried when she saw it."

Miss Porterfield waited, nodding.

"Seven, perhaps, it had gotten dark, but I can't remember if it was a coming storm or just the night. It was so long ago, you know."

Miss Porterfield nodded slightly as she listened hard to another question. She looked across time at the curious.

"Well, yes," said Miss Porterfield. "I think so."

Benetsee nodded. He touched Du Pré on the arm and he raised his fingers and was gone.

Du Pré heard the car door open and then slam again. Pelon had gotten out and they would have vanished by now.

Miss Porterfield dabbed at her eyes.

"It was so terrible," she said, she looked up, her eyes brimmed.

"That's really all that I know," said Miss Porterfield. "Could I get you some more tea?"

Du Pré waited.

Miss Porterfield sat demurely, back straight, head a little down.

She raised her right arm and she held it straight out from her shoulder. She pressed her hand against the wall.

Her arm began to tremble, a vibration, then a shaking, then her hand flew around, jerking on the end of her nerves.

167

She pressed her head back hard against the wall.

Her eyes rolled up in her head and her whole body shook, her tongue was thrust out and her jaws clenched as she bit it.

Blood ran down her chin and cheek and on to her hair.

She shook for a time and then she went limp and slumped down, but she didn't fall.

A knock at the door.

"Come in Bart," yelled Du Pré.

He waited.

"Oh, my God," said Bart. "We have to give her CPR."

He started toward her.

Du Pré grabbed him.

"No," he said. "Her time is now."

"Jesus," said Bart, "I can smell the goddamned brandy."

Du Pré nodded.

"It is here," he said. "You maybe go, call Benny, they will have to take her."

"What's here?" said Bart.

Du Pré shook his head and Bart pulled out his little cell phone.

Du Pré walked over to the torn photograph.

Albert Messmer, Genevette, and their four children, dark 'breed faces, round and young.

Messmer wore the crude clothes of a cattleman, his beard and hair were long and greasy.

Genevette was incredibly beautiful, dark-eyed, heart-shaped face, her braids wrapped in otterskins, her slender hands together as though she was praying.

Du Pré looked at the little torn photograph.

"Benny's on his way," said Bart. "Say, what's that?"

Du Pré handed the photo to him.

"Who is it?" said Bart.

Du Pré took the photo back and he put it in his pocket.

"It is Genevette," said Du Pré, "with that Albert Messmer and their four children."

Bart looked down at the floor.

"This belongs to somebody," said Du Pré. "Him come for it."

They went outside to wait for Benny.

✦ CHAPTER 30 ✦

"Madelaine she is fine," said Bassman. "She say for you to hurry up."

Du Pré nodded.

Yeah, I just figure this out, shoot a few people, everything is ver' quiet. Nothing makes sense. That Miss Porterfield she just up and die, seizures, and Benetsee he is gone again. That Messmer ranch they are doing something, can't find it.

Some warrior running in the night, let him go, maybe that take care of it.

"This music maybe is better than the last time," said Du Pré.

The Dead Day.

"Day like that," said Bassman, "God is at the dentist, root canal, don't got His mind on His job."

Bassman slid open the van door. He grabbed his amplifier and humped it up the steps of the Toussaint Saloon's porch and set it down.

"You," said Bassman. "You think too much maybe. That blonde she go back to Minneapolis, her husband. She don't think enough."

Du Pré snorted. He grabbed an aluminum suitcase with the cords and mikes in it and a heavy flat sound board cased in black phony leather.

Susan Klein was sitting on a high stool behind the bar, mouth tight, staring at her beadwork.

"You want drinks," she said, "you get 'em. Serious art goin' on here."

"Poor Benny," said Bassman. "Had a wife, now he got an *artist*."

"Poor Bassman," said Susan Klein. "He used to get paid but now he works for free."

Bassman grinned. Susan didn't look up.

The summer's middle heat had started. It was a hundred degrees out and the sky was white with dust.

Sweat plenty here tonight, Du Pré thought.

Some time, I can tell it will be good music, good crowd, good time. That will be tonight.

"Bassman," said Susan, "whose wife you got in the van this time?"

"Hillary Clinton," said Bassman, "but she don't inhale."

"Du Pré," said Susan, "where did you find this animal?"

"Zoo," said Du Pré. "Toss him a banana, him follow me home."

Bassman grinned and he went back out to the van.

Du Pré went behind the bar and he fixed himself a drink and pulled a beer for Bassman.

"Shame about poor old Miss Porterfield," said Susan Klein. "Benny was so sad about her."

Du Pré nodded.

"I push booze here," said Susan. "Sometimes I wonder how many of my friends and neighbors I'm killin'."

"No one," said Du Pré. "You are killing no one."

"I still wonder," said Susan.

"Everybody die," said Du Pré. "They got to pick how, too."

Susan nodded.

"I expect so," she said.

Du Pré sipped his drink. Bassman was sucking on a spliff outside and when he was done he would come in dry-throated and want his beer. Then they could set up.

Père Godin was up at the little church, confessing his crimes of reproductive genius to Father Van Den Heuvel.

"Thanks, Du Pré," said Susan Klein. "I guess I was just sad about Miss Porterfield. She was a funny old thing with a good heart."

Du Pré nodded.

Maybe not. I look on the floor of her little pickup, it got a few beads on it. One of them beads is the red kind, pret' rare, tires are the kind made them tracks, let the guy out cut Messmer in half with a shotgun.

Maybe I don't want to know, let it work it out some.

"Benny's afraid you'll do something crazy, Du Pré," said Susan. "It bothers him?"

"Me?" said Du Pré.

"Christ," said Susan Klein. "Never mind. There are going to be a lot of people here tonight. I got a rule of thumb, I get two calls, it means twelve more people for dinner, I put another prime rib in the oven. The oven has all the prime rib it can hold now, and it's a big damn oven."

Du Pré waited.

"Sure wish Madelaine was here," said Susan.

"Yah," said Du Pré.

Du Pré went out to his cruiser and he got his fiddle case and the old bow case with the MP-40 and the two spare magazines.

He looked up the street toward the little church.

Père Godin was walking toward the saloon, standing up a little more erectly, no longer bowed down by the weight of his sins.

Father Van Den Heuvel came out of the church. He glanced at Du Pré. He looked heavenward and he spread his hands palm up. Then he grinned.

Du Pré laughed.

He went on in.

Du Pré set the bow case behind Bassman's big amp.

Père Godin came in carrying his accordion case and lighter soul.

"Ah, Du Pré," said Père Godin, "that Father Van Den Heuvel he is a fine priest, him." Père Godin was a connoisseur of confessions and a good judge of priest's hearts.

Du Pré laughed.

The band ate early and Du Pré drove on out to Bart's with Bassman to sleep a little. Susan Klein had said they should start at ten rather than nine. The summer light was long and people came to dinner later and there were a hell of a lot of them on the way.

Du Pré awoke when Bassman snored so loud that the little chimes on Bart's mantelpiece rang faintly. They were on the couches. The light was at a deep angle and it stabbed across the room, dust gold and swirling in it.

They drove back to the bar and found the place jammed with people eating and talking. Some young cowboys were across the street in the little park, cheering on two who were pounding on each other.

Benny Klein, still in uniform, was pulling drinks and shoving them across the bar to the women waiting on the tables and Susan was ranging up and down the length of the old walnut slab keeping everyone topped off.

The CLOSED sign came on over the door to the kitchen.

Her run out of meat, Du Pré thought, this crowd maybe eat us, too.

Crowd you got to make hungry and then feed, Catfoot had said, they are your guests, your heart, you treat them well. Don't be too drunk, just some drunk. Fiddler who is too drunk, plays bad, insults the guests.

Susan had guessed well and every one of the tables had dirty plates on it and satisfied people in the chairs.

Du Pré helped clear the tables, running back and forth to the big sinks in the kitchen with gray tubs full of crockery and silverware and glasses. Susan and Benny's teen-aged daughters were there washing up like hell.

Du Pré finished one last load and then he went to the stage and he got his fiddle out. Bassman was there, reeking of burnt hemp, his dark glasses on, his worn black leather coat, and a crimson silk shirt. Red River Man.

Père Godin chuffled through some chords on his old accordion. Du Pré held his fiddle to his ear and he plucked the strings, pret' good, only one a little flat.

Thump thump thump. Bassman's slap bass runs, somewhere between big strings and a drum.

The people in the crowd whistled and stomped on the floor. The old building shook a little.

Du Pré started off with the "Black River Paddle Song," for the voyageurs pulling like hell on the paddles to make way with the big freighter canoe as it shot down the rapids other voyageurs were too cowardly to try.

We are back at the factory with our pelts drinking rum while you who have not a ball among you carry your packs and canoes around all the water that scares you. Hah.

We are Métis, we die we are cheerful, hello God, You got that good rum, pipes, tobacco? You don't. You are rude, we paddle on, find somebody with manners here, heaven.

They finished and went right on, war songs, buffalo hunt songs, cart songs, and then Du Pré slowed things down with the "Song of Genevette." Genevette walking with her frozen feet through the snow with her sledful of babies, looking for the Métis camp. A slow walking song.

People got up and danced, you could two-step to it.

Du Pré opened his eyes near the song's end. Jerry Jacquot was on the dance floor with a woman, someone Du Pré didn't know. They turned and Du Pré gave a start and almost dropped rhythm.

Shannon Smiley, the woman with Bongo and the other guy, in here so briefly.

Du Pré watched them dance to the back of the room near the door. The crowd closed in front of them and the smoke thick as deep fog ate the light.

When the set ended Du Pré wiped his fiddle strings with a soft cloth and then his face. He grabbed a tall whiskey and water and went out the front door.

A lot of couples had come outside, trading one kind of heat for another.

Du Pré swallowed big gulps of his cold drink.

They are not here.

What is this?

CHAPTER 31

G oddamn it, Du Pré," said Harvey, "you know I can't comment on that. Just leave it alone."

"You want to know anyone see that Smiley woman, that Willie
Beeton guy," said Du Pré. "So I do and I call you."

"It is four A.M. here," said Harvey, "in Washington, D.C. I am
glad to know Shannon Smiley is there. Nothing to be done,
though, charges were dropped in that Sacramento thing."

"Okay," said Du Pré.

"The witness had a change of heart," said Harvey, "or part of
one. Somebody cut it out, anyway."

"Huh?" said Du Pré.

"Somebody sawed out the girl's pump," said Harvey. "I keep
telling you these people play very rough."

"This Jerry Jacquot is one, your guys?" said Du Pré.

"Nope," said Harvey. "Scout's honor. Yale. Champion gymnast,
you know, they wanted him for the Olympic team but he said he
liked gymnastics well enough but not enough to make a career of
it. Smart guy. So he's out there with one of the little Martin
princes, being a cowboy a while."

"We don't get a picture," said Du Pré. "It is too crowded they
are not near enough to that owl for the camera to see them."

"Can I go back to bed now?" said Harvey. "I'm old and need
my rest."

"Prick," said Du Pré.

"Ripper should be there about tomorrow," said Harvey. "Said he wanted to check a couple things out."

Du Pré hung up.

Lying sack of shit.

That damn Jerry Jacquot is one of his guys, little bastard is too many places not to be.

Or he wears moccasins, waits at Benetsee's, strangles Bongo.

Maybe he is not one of Harvey's.

So maybe that is even better.

Maybe he got a red bead stuck, his shoe.

The door to Bart's room was shut. He hadn't been at the Toussaint Saloon that night, but then sometimes he didn't come if he was down and did not want to see people.

Du Pré went to bed. He slept hard and didn't wake up until Bart came in with a big cup of coffee.

"You got company," said Bart.

Du Pré swung his legs over the side of the bed and he shook his head and he sucked down some scalding coffee and pulled on his pants and socks and boots and stretched; he shrugged into a shirt and went into the bathroom and splashed cold water on his face.

He looked at himself.

Old Métis shit-brain fiddle player. I find a young guy, let him do this shit.

"Goooooooooodddddd mooooorrrrrnnnnnninnnnnnng," said Ripper when Du Pré came out to the big living room. "Great-Aunt Harvey sends his best and hopes you'll let him sleep from now on. He actually *whined*. It must be hell to be old as you guys."

"What you want?" asked Du Pré.

"Well," said Ripper, "I don't really know. I thought you might help me. Harvey said something about an old medicine man. He also said something about go fix this and just do it."

Du Pré nodded.

"That Smiley woman she is in the bar last night," said Du Pré.

"So I hear," said Ripper. "Shannon is a real peach. Does paid hits. Most of the paid-hit folks are women. Who is going to suspect a lady jogger or some stern-looking nanny pushing a baby carriage?"

"Jesus," said Du Pré.

"Shannon, well," said Ripper. "One I liked best was this asshole had ripped off her club, there, of some pounds of heroin, and was holed up on the top floor of a hotel in Vegas, with a lot of good friends around he knows and who have guns and mean eyes, don't trust anybody."

"So Shannon shows up, somehow she gets tapped to come on up, give this guy a nice blowjob, maybe the rest of the crew. They search her, her bag, she's a junkie, got her works with her, she gets them all off and while she's in the asshole's bathroom brushing her teeth and gargling she swaps her works for his, goes out in the room and shoots up, courtesy these assholes who are grateful. She leaves, with free dope and a wad of hundred-dollar bills, thanks from these guys."

"Shannon's long gone, like ten minutes, and the asshole needs a fix, goes into the bathroom and shoots up and his buddies hear a thud in there and they rush in and watch the guy die. Whatever she put in the works is pretty mean, too, guy has an awful time of it."

"Works are needles?" said Du Pré.

"Indeed," said Ripper. "Pardon my rudeness in using jargon, us white boys do that just to sound tough. Anyway. By that evening all the heroin that was ripped off had been restored to the rightful owners, along with heartfelt apologies and a suitcase full of money. She's good, I give her that."

"She is not wanted no more?" said Du Pré.

"Nope," said Ripper. "I am sure Harvey told you, somebody sawed out the witness's heart. Probably ate it, too. Most crooks are just plain dumb, but these bastards are cruel and smart. We hate them a lot."

"Okay," said Du Pré. "What you want?"

"I'd just love to go out to the Martins and chat up Jerry Jacquot," said Ripper. "I've been meaning to make his acquaintance."

Du Pré nodded. The Martins had been very civil even if Du Pré had had some part in the deaths of two of them.

"Okay," said Du Pré.

"Of course," said Ripper, "if you are uncomfortable going there, and could arrange some sort of introduction, I would wing it, you know."

Du Pré shook his head.

"I take you," he said.

Maybe we help each other.

Du Pré called. Mrs. Martin's secretary went off the line for a moment and then she came back on and said that tea would be served at ten.

Tea. Christ.

"We see them, ten," said Du Pré.

"Good," said Ripper. "Now how 'bout some more coffee? I didn't get to sleep last night, too busy flying and driving. I say this only to prove how devoted I am to my job."

Bart pointed to the coffeemaker. Ripper went to it and filled his cup.

"That Harvey say you float down the Amazon, a kayak," said Du Pré.

"Did too," said Ripper. "Started out that way, anyhow. Youthful folly."

"Alone?" said Du Pré.

179

"Ah, no," said Ripper. "There were four of us actually, thought we'd have a little adventure before life got dull."

He looked down into his coffee cup.

"I made it home," he said. "The others didn't."

Du Pré nodded.

"We were doing fine but then we blundered into a nest of pirates," said Ripper. "They were stealing the gold miners' stuff and killing them, there on the river."

Pirates. Christ.

"There wasn't any warning," said Ripper, his voice softer, "and I lived because a snake had dropped into my kayak and I was behind and getting the damn thing out. Just a little boa, no big deal, but you know how it is trying to paddle in a kayak with a snake in there."

Du Pré waited.

"So I hear shotgun blasts. I knew what had happened. We had a shotgun and a rifle with us but it wasn't one of them, I knew that, the shotgun was just a twenty-gauge, was all. So there were maybe a dozen shots and then there were three. Very methodical those last three. They were shooting my friends in the head one last time to make sure. So I hid and slipped past in the night and headed downriver. All the navigation gear was in another kayak. But I did have a lot of food."

Du Pré waited.

"It rained," said Ripper. "It rained for days, weeks. It never quit. It rained hard and the rivers rose way up and flooded the land and they weren't rivers any more. Everything was a lake. I couldn't tell where I was. No current to see. No stars. I got fungus all over, it ate at my skin. The rain quit and the rivers fell and I could go on. The holes in my skin got infected. I found a port on the river. There was one nurse there. She put poultices on my ulcers for three months and they finally healed. I went on and out and came home."

Bart was looking at Ripper.

"So that was my big adventure," said Ripper, "which it surely was."

"So you go to work for Harvey," said Du Pré.

"Yeah," said Ripper. "My dad and Harvey are friends, sort of, and I was sort of drinking a lot and sleeping too much. So I am out in the backyard in a stupor and Harvey comes over, chews my ass out, says he could use some good help. Here'n I thought I'd maybe spend my life as a banker, like dad."

Du Pré laughed.

They went out to the old cruiser.

Ripper slapped his hand on the roof a few times while he looked up at the mountains and then he got in.

✤ CHAPTER 32 ✤

Du Pré and Ripper were ushered into Morgan Martin's conservatory by her secretary, a handsome woman in her fifties dressed as though she was in Manhattan rather than a part of Montana so remote paved roads were few and far between.

The erect old woman sat at a marble-topped table, cut flowers in a huge vase in front of her. A samovar stood on a brass cart, liquor bottles arrayed underneath.

"This is . . ." said Du Pré, ". . . Ripper."

"Charles Van Dusen," said Ripper.

Morgan Martin motioned them to sit. She kept her eyes on Ripper.

"You're one of Bella Simms' people," she said. It was not a question.

"Quite," said Ripper. "Second cousin, I think."

"Are you the one that got into that dreadful trouble in Peru?" asked Morgan Martin.

"Brazil," said Ripper.

"Brazil, then," said Morgan Martin, "you young folk. Two of one of my classmate's sons were . . . they wanted to see gorillas, took a wrong turn, and ended up getting eaten. Some rebel army, did that sort of thing."

Du Pré looked up at the ceiling.

"The Pollard boys," said Ripper. "Couple years ahead of me at school."

"Dreadful business," said Morgan Martin. "Still, adventure calls. Now, you do something in government?"

"FBI," said Ripper.

"Your mother must be having fits," said Morgan Martin. "State or perhaps Treasury would have been more suitable, I should think."

"I did not come out here to take crap from some insufferable old broad in the matter of what I choose to do in life," said Ripper. "Now might I have a cup? Milk, no sugar."

Morgan Martin beamed.

"Of course," she said. "Forgive me, Mr. Du Pré, I did need to know what manner of man was here asking questions about our guest."

Du Pré shrugged. Somebody tapped his shoulder lightly. It was the secretary. She held out a tall glass of whiskey and ice and water.

Morgan Martin poured tea in big cups. She added milk and handed the cup to Ripper. She had none herself.

"Tribal nonsense," said Morgan Martin. "Mr. Du Pré is a humorist, I expect a song out of this."

No shit, thought Du Pré looking at the ceiling.

"Paul and Jerry are out riding," said Morgan Martin, "but I expect them back momentarily."

"Who is Jerry, exactly?" asked Ripper.

"Haven't a clue," said Morgan Martin, "save that he is not one of those little rich shits no better than they should be."

"I'm sure you know that we are interested in what is going on at the Messmer place," said Ripper.

"Thugs," said Morgan Martin. "Up to no good. Dope, I'm sure."

"No doubt," said Ripper.

Male voices sounded in the back hall.

Paul Martin and Jerry Jacquot came in. They were dressed in jeans and boots and hats. Their faces were a little flushed.

"Charles here had some reason for meeting you, Jerry," said Morgan Martin.

Jerry looked puzzled.

"Oh, really?" he said.

"This tribal crap is getting on my nerves," said Ripper, "so why don't you and me take a walk. Du Pré can sit here doubled over in amusement at our little ways."

"Charles is with the FBI," said Morgan Martin, "and he seems to like it well enough."

Ripper stood up. He looked at Jerry Jacquot.

"I think," said Jerry, "that perhaps Mr. Du Pré should join us."

"Right," said Ripper. "Wouldn't think of not having him."

Paul Martin sat down next to his grandmother.

Jerry Jacquot turned and headed back the way he had come.

Ripper and Du Pré followed.

Jerry led them down a long hall and into a guest room that looked out on the western range of the Wolf Mountains.

"And?" he said.

"And you've been in and out of the Messmer ranch and you surely saw a few things," said Ripper. "And I surely do not give a shit about certain matters you wouldn't talk about anyway."

Jerry Jacquot looked at him.

"I'm interested in the place," he said.

"God," said Ripper, "don't make me do this."

"Do what?" said Jerry Jacquot, smiling. "Threaten me?"

"We are after them," said Ripper, "because they are not nice and they are making up one hell of a lot of methamphetamine somewhere around here and we can't spot it."

"Meth?" said Jerry Jacquot.

"You were not dancing cheek to cheek with Shannon Smiley

because she smells good," said Ripper. "Now you know what she *does* in life?"

Jerry Jacquot held his palms up.

"She kills people," said Ripper.

"Appalling," said Jerry Jacquot. "Why don't you arrest her?"

Ripper looked at Du Pré.

"You see what I have to contend with?" he said. "Harvey'd have the cuffs on him and be kicking him in the ribs by now. Maybe I'll try that."

"Ripper, it is, I think?" said Jerry Jacquot. "I haven't any idea of what it is you would like from me."

"How 'bout you don't get killed," said Ripper. "That would be good, and maybe you just get on a plane and the fuck out of here, would be good, too, very, very good."

"Research," said Jerry Jacquot. "Writing a book, you know. Always interested, you stay alive longer. It's the real truth I seek."

Du Pré rolled a smoke and lit it.

"The old woman who just croaked," said Ripper, "what's she to you?"

"Miss Porterfield was an historian," said Jerry Jacquot, "Kind enough to leave her materials to me. Right there in the will. You could look it up."

"I will," said Ripper, "but you need to get out of here."

"Can't," said Jacquot. "Onward march of scholarship."

"That goddamned place is cameras and motion sensors and the like," said Ripper. "You've been in there."

"Just to drop off Miss Smiley last night," said Jerry Jacquot.

"You met her at the saloon?" said Ripper.

"I was running," said Jerry Jacquot, "keeping the old circulation going. She was kind enough to pick me up and give me a ride."

"Very nice," said Ripper. "I really believe that, since she was on her way to take out Du Pré."

Du Pré looked at Ripper.

"No shit," he said. "I mean it." Ripper held up his hand, scout's honor.

"She was most pleasant," said Jerry Jacquot.

"No doubt," said Ripper.

"Why would she be interested in killing Mr. Du Pré?" said Jerry.

"This conversation," said Ripper, "is going nowhere."

"Where would you like it to go, Mr. . . . Van Dusen, is it?"

"Van Dusen it is and *those* Van Dusens to boot," said Ripper. "We need something. You have to have seen *something.*"

"Well," said Jerry Jacquot, "why didn't you say so. I did see something unusual."

"I liked it better back when I could pull out fingernails," said Ripper.

"Fumes," said Jerry Jacquot. "I saw fumes."

"Fumes," said Ripper.

"Yup," said Jerry Jacquot.

"And where were these fumes?" said Ripper.

"Curling out of a metal building," said Jerry Jacquot.

"How nice," said Jerry Jacquot. "They smell like ether? Petrochemicals?"

"Nope," said Jerry Jacquot, "didn't."

"Fuck me to death," said Ripper. "Ammonia. We never thought of that."

"Sure did," said Jerry Jacquot.

"We can go now," said Ripper.

"Glad to be of help," said Jerry Jacquot.

Ripper grabbed Du Pré's arm and pulled him along out the front door.

"Drive!" he screamed.

Du Pré headed down the long drive and he turned toward Bart's place.

"So this Shannon woman she is here, try to kill me?" said Du Pré.

"Don't worry about it," said Ripper.

"Me, I worry," said Du Pré.

Ripper looked over at him.

"She's dead," he said, "is what she is."

❖ CHAPTER 33 ❖

They look too small to be riding those big horses," said Raymond. He leaned on his crutches, already tired. The walk to the car and the drive and the walk to the big corral had already exhausted him.

Berne and Marisa were riding full tilt around and around the corral on a pair of quarter horses. They shrieked with joy.

When Du Pré had said that he would look for some ponies both little girls set up wails.

Ponies! We are horse riders! We will be grown up soon, have to feed ponies, the dogs! No ponies!

Du Pré looked at Raymond. Tired, aching, his breaks healing, his little daughters about to snap their necks. He looked very proud.

"Them ride good," he said. He smiled.

"I take you to the car you sit, rest," said Du Pré. "I take you home come back for these savages."

"Me," said Raymond. "All these kids, me I feel like them Jesuit, come here, the heathens. Ver' patient, them Jesuit."

Du Pré walked back to the old cruiser with him. He was near but careful not to touch Raymond, even when Raymond stumbled a little. Leave him his pride.

"Get that damn stirrup back you little walloper!" hollered Booger Tom. "Yer ridin' like a . . . em . . . uh . . . environmentalist!"

Raymond and Du Pré turned and looked back at the old cowboy.

"Yah," said Raymond, "he is a good man, so he doesn't swear around my daughters. Worse thing he can say is 'vironmentalist. That's pret' bad." He laughed.

Booger Tom he is looking for a cuss word, all the way through his collection, like some old woman looking for the right button in a jar.

Du Pré opened the door of the old cruiser for Raymond and he held it so Raymond would have something to grab when he needed to lower himself down.

Raymond slumped back in the seat. His face was pale.

"I take you home come back for them," said Du Pré. "That Booger Tom he is there, Bart's guards, they will be all right."

Raymond nodded. Du Pré walked back over to Booger Tom.

"Raymond is tired," said Du Pré. "I drive him home, come back, you watch them?"

Booger Tom nodded.

"Little blisters," said Booger Tom. "Hell on wheels, ain't they?"

Du Pré laughed.

The little girls were glued to their saddles, heads down, yelping with joy.

Du Pré walked back to his cruiser and got in and drove off down the long drive; he turned on to the bench road and headed for Toussaint.

He passed a woman with a geologist's pick and a musette bag who was sitting by a dull outcrop of mudstone like a million others. The outcrop had a fine view of everywhere about.

Du Pré lifted three fingers off the steering wheel and waved with them one time. The woman grinned.

Bart's people ver' thorough, Du Pré thought.

The Messmer ranch had been so quiet. No visitors, no long

horse trailers arriving and departing. The hands and Kelleher went about their business, the ordinary chores of ranching.

Too quiet.

They got worse things to think about now than me, Du Pré thought.

Jacqueline came out when Du Pré pulled up, and several children, too. The little ones stood in a group by the gate, waiting.

Du Pré held the door and Raymond struggled upright and got his crutches under his arms. Jacqueline just put her hand lightly on his shoulder.

Du Pré's youngest grandchildren moved toward him in a body. Little Alcide, five years old, was in front.

"Grand-père," said Alcide, trying to be grave and mature, "we would like ver' much to know when we could maybe ride horses."

Du Pré looked at the little boy.

"Marifa and Berne get to ride howths," said little Pallas, four. She had trouble with sibilants.

Little heads nodded at one another. Established fact.

"Marisa and Berne they eat their vegetables, wash their faces, brush teeth," said Du Pré.

"Bullfit," said Pallas. "Them feed damn vegattables the dogs. Put them in this sack they got, the table under."

Massed cries of affirmation.

Shit. Thought Du Pré.

"Okay," said Du Pré, "maybe you talk, your mother, this."

"More bullfit," said Pallas. "She say talk to you."

My lovely daughter, the bitch, thought Du Pré.

Think fast, Grand-père.

"I think about it, let you know tonight, maybe after dinner," said Du Pré.

Happy little faces.

Pallas beamed.

She got me now, Du Pré thought.

Maybe I move, Canada, send word, I am dead.

Du Pré slunk back to his cruiser. He rolled a smoke and lit it and he headed back to Bart's.

Booger Tom was still leaned up against the fencepost. His hat was pushed back. A part-circle of white shone on his forehead, brilliant against the deep red-brown of his face.

"The one in front took a spill," said Booger Tom. "Said she weren't hurt but she was lyin'."

Du Pré nodded. Kid is really hurt they are unconscious. They move they squall, they are all right mostly.

Marisa was bobbing a little too much.

Du Pré stepped through the corral poles and he held up his hand.

The well-trained cow ponies slowed and stopped and walked up to him.

Marisa grinned at her grandfather, but her little eyes were tight with pain.

"You fall," said Du Pré.

"Yes, Grand-père," said Marisa. She looked sick.

Du Pré lifted her off and carried her toward the gate.

Berne slid down and trotted after.

"I'll get them horses," said Booger Tom, swinging the gate open.

Du Pré nodded.

"Grand-père," said Marisa, "I am sorry. You won't make me not ride horses, will you?"

"What you break?" said Du Pré, after he had set Marisa on the seat and Berne had scrambled in the back door.

"My arm," said Marisa, in a tiny voice.

Du Pré felt with his fingers.

Broken all right, but not busted through the skin.

He got a big cotton kerchief from the trunk of the car and he made a sling to take the weight off and ease the pain.

Marisa was crying but she wouldn't make any sound. Tears fell down her little cheeks.

Du Pré drove like hell for Cooper and the clinic. The young doctor's SUV was there. He picked up Marisa and he ran inside.

The doctor and a couple of nurses were working on someone laid out on a gurney. No one looked up.

Du Pré sat and waited with the little girls.

He heard a helicopter in the distance. It got closer and then it came down right outside the clinic.

The doctor and the nurses began to wheel the gurney out. The IV fluids danced on their hooks.

Du Pré got up and he watched the medical team from the helicopter take over, and slide the patient into the bay. The team jumped back in and then the helicopter lifted off and then the jet engines kicked on.

Cheaper to buy a fast helicopter than keep open all the little hospitals.

The doctor and the nurses came back in. One nurse was crying and shuddering. The doctor spoke to her and she nodded and went off toward the coffee room. The other nurse was older and her face was set.

"What you got?" said the doctor.

"She break her arm," said Du Pré.

"Hazard of being a kid," said the doctor. He knelt in front of Marisa and he talked while he felt gently for the fracture.

"Looks like you get a cast," said the doctor.

"A light one," said Marisa. "I got to ride. It is my life."

"Okay, cowgirl," said the doctor. "One light cast coming up. Got to take a X-ray."

192

He picked up Marisa and carried her back to the X-ray room.

Du Pré got cans of pop for himself and Berne. The little girl excused herself and she went off to the bathroom.

Du Pré walked to the coffee room.

The young nurse was staring off into a far country.

"What was that?" said Du Pré.

The nurse looked at him, startled.

"Somebody cut that woman's face off," said the nurse.

She went back to staring.

♣ CHAPTER 34 ♣

Du Pré stood in the huge front hall of the Martin house, looking at his face in the smoky pierglass. The mirror was courteous and flattering to guests. Du Pré looked thirty years younger. The reflection was a soft, smooth, and cosmetic face.

Boot heels sounded crisply on the pegged oak floor. A carpet muffled them and then they began again, closer.

"Ah, Du Pré," said Morgan Martin, "I knew you would return. I even considered leaving suddenly for Paris or Rome. But that would not help, would it."

Du Pré shrugged.

"Other day, I am here," said Du Pré, "you say maybe I write a song about you, Ripper, way you people do your lives."

Morgan Martin looked coolly at Du Pré.

"The rich are like everyone else," she said, "mostly bad. So what have you found to skewer, Mr. Du Pré?"

"No," said Du Pré. "But me, I think of a song, maybe. I like to play, sing it for you."

Young men laughed far off in the house, a door slammed.

Morgan Martin looked at Du Pré for a long time.

"The conservatory is being cleaned now," she said, "but the greenhouse is pleasant."

She mean orangerie, Du Pré thought, what we Métis call them, too.

No Métis ever raise a damn orange, though.

Morgan Martin walked away, taking firm little steps.

Du Pré followed, carrying the old fiddle in its old case.

Morgan went through several rooms and then a dining room, a formal one with a table that could seat thirty, silver candelabra set on bright white lace. A tall sideboard glowed with liquor bottles and a narrow door next to it had a long window running down the middle. The light was on in the room, and Du Pré could see wine in racks.

They went through a huge kitchen, full of stainless steel and giant blackened cast-iron stoves and chopping blocks set on wheels. Pans and pots by the dozens hung from hooks over the center island.

It was four times as big as the kitchen at the Toussaint Saloon.

Morgan Martin went through a heavy door, one that was dutched so the top half could be opened.

"It's a pleasant day," said Morgan Martin. "Would you please fix the top of the door open for me?"

Du Pré undid the latch and he hooked the top half back and he pulled the bottom shut.

The greenhouse was a good hundred feet long and thirty wide and filled with plants.

Morgan Martin found a director's chair and she unfolded it and she turned.

"I was being a jackass," she said. "I apologize."

Du Pré laughed.

Open that door, she tells me, so that you know you are a servant.

"I see a cow I look at the brand," said Du Pré. "I am not a brand inspector years now, maybe part-time, but I still look. I am like that."

"And I, alas, am like *that*," said Morgan Martin.

Her husband is dead, her sons are dead, and I help kill them,

195

Du Pré thought, she can't stop things but she live to see them done right anyway.

"Would you like a drink, Mr. Du Pré?" said Morgan Martin. She got up. "A musician must have his courtesies given."

Du Pré nodded.

She tapped off back into the house.

Du Pré set down the fiddle case and he walked up and down the rows of plants, he looked into the misted room where strange trailing plants with thick weird blooms lived.

Bay laurel trees, herbs, a lemon tree, cut low and tight, with fat small lemons on it.

Du Pré turned when he heard Morgan Martin coming back. He walked over to where they had been and he took the tall glass from her and he sniffed.

"Just bourbon," said Morgan Martin. "I know that I cannot fight you. Artists are the most powerful people of all, Mr. Du Pré, though they are usually poor and troubled. They find the rich and we pay them off, but there is no escape from them for us."

Du Pré laughed. He sipped his drink.

She invite me here, play fiddle, she is burying her two sons that I help kill. I play some, sad songs, black forests and dead warriors, and then a bagpiper, he plays off in the trees where no one can see him.

Du Pré took out his fiddle and he tuned it and he then tuned his bow. He cut a loose horsehair. He drew the bow over the strings and they sang.

Du Pré played the song of Genevette, sometimes standing with the fiddle and bow loose in his hands and singing a verse before bowing the chorus.

Morgan Martin was looking off to a far country and her eyes shone.

Du Pré did a round of the chorus and he let his keening wail and the violin die away together.

Morgan Martin said nothing. Then she got up and she walked back to the house and she came back with another tall drink for Du Pré and she had a balloon glass with a lot of brandy in it.

"My French is good," said Morgan Martin, "if I am in Paris. What is it you call your sort of French?"

"Metchif'," said Du Pré, "coyote French."

"The verbs are what?" said Morgan Martin, "Indian?"

"Cree," said Du Pré, "some Cree anyway. I think."

"Genevette was sent off through the snow to make way for Messmer's white wife?" said Morgan Martin.

Du Pré nodded.

"These songs they come to me," said Du Pré. "I don't know how but they explain, every new story is old, you know?"

Morgan Martin nodded.

"So I got this other song," said Du Pré, "maybe a better song."

Du Pré drank a long pull from his drink. The words to the song ran fast, parts of verses, the high points.

There was a wooden soft drink crate under the table. Du Pré moved it out with his boot. He stood on it. An old one, strong enough to take his weight.

Du Pré got up on it and he began to tap his right foot.

He did this for a while and then he bowed his fiddle and let one long note go on and on.

The song was a war song, about a man named Red Hawk With Yellow Feathers when he was with the Sioux, and the Métis making war, and Red Hawk With Yellow Feathers was a brave warrior, crazy brave.

He could steal horses from under Sioux riders and leave them dead and scalped and mutilated so they would have to walk the

Star Trail all ashamed, because the mutilations are carried by the ghost, too.

Red Hawk With Yellow Feathers once charged a war party all alone and he was so brave and made the ululation so well the Sioux were panicked and they fled.

Red Hawk With Yellow Feathers would dance sometimes, dance so well, graceful as a cat, with a cat's speed and balance.

But back in the camps, where the Red River carts stood in front of the teepees and the Métis lived on the buffalo grounds, he had another life and he did the work of a wife for a man, his man.

Red Hawk With Yellow Feathers, bravest of the brave.

He was a bardache, a man who was a brave warrior in battle, but who did woman's work in the camp. He beaded beautifully, and prepared good food, and kept clean, and made fine clothes for his man.

Du Pré sang the song through and he let the fiddle and bow down and he tapped his foot and slowed the tempo and he stopped and he got down and he pushed the crate back where it had been.

Morgan Martin had her hands on her face.

"All right," she said. "What do I have to do now?"

Du Pré leaned back on the table.

"Jerry, him bardache," said Du Pré. "He save my life maybe two times. So I owe him, maybe, my life."

Morgan Martin looked up at Du Pré.

"They've been together three years," she said. "They love each other."

Du Pré nodded.

"Him got a song," he said. "His mother's best friend she is killed. He remembers. He gets older he finds out, he learns that song, Genevette."

"I don't know when it started," said Morgan Martin.

"It start a century, more, ago," said Du Pré.

"How did you know?" said Morgan Martin.

Du Pré walked to the raspberry bushes in their bed. He picked some and he crushed them in his hand. He opened his palm, red.

"I still don't know what you want me to do," said Morgan Martin.

"Him going," said Du Pré. "Him go in a week, and I drive him down, we go alone."

Morgan Martin nodded.

"This song," said Du Pré, "it don't need too many verses, you know?"

Morgan Martin got up.

"They will listen to me," she said.

Du Pré nodded and he left.

✤ CHAPTER 35 ✤

A untie, let me drive," said Ripper. "I think he needs a big bowl of downers."

"Ignore the little prick," said Harvey Wallace. "He'll go away and go to law school and chisel the rest of his life like God intended."

"Been to law school," said Ripper. "Dull. I like all this excitement. Cloaks. Daggers. Forces of Evil."

"What is wrong with the goddamned CIA then?" said Harvey. "Why us?"

"The CIA," said Ripper, "is where good families send their sons who are far too stupid to trust with the family brokerage."

"That explains a lot," said Harvey.

"Sure does," said Ripper. "I have two idiot cousins work there. Every time I see a goddamned flag burning, the old red, white, and blue, on the news, I know what desk Chess and Jack have been transferred to. I don't even have to *ask*."

"I think your family liked the FBI idea so much," said Harvey, "because there was hope you'd get killed."

"Harvey's in a pissy mood, Du Pré," said Ripper. "God, listen to him *whine*."

They were sitting in a car eighty miles from Toussaint, at a rail yard built for wheat and now used to process fertilizer for ranchers.

There were fifty cops, state troopers, sheriff's deputies, and some technicians swarming over the whole installation.

A small tank farm and a processing works and a chain-link yard for delivery trucks.

The men who worked there were standing in a huddle off by the shabby trailer that served as an office. A man in a suit was asking them a few questions.

"They were smarter than we were, Harv," said Ripper, "for a while anyway. 'Course we're so nice we take time to think bad thoughts, like they do."

"It's the simple stuff fucks you up," said Harvey. "They get the liquid ammonia here, just steal it and pay some dink to falsify the records, clear back at the headquarters, process the stuff cold at the Messmer place and ship it out with the horses. Neat. The shit goes into the lake. Very smart."

Du Pré snorted. He didn't understand a lot of it.

"Methamphetamine, crank, speed, about fifty other cute in-crowd names," said Ripper. "Big profit margin. Dangerous to process, though. Gets a lot less dangerous you got liquid ammonia at minus two hundred and four point three degrees. Run the waste products out in the lake at night and it is all gone by the morning."

The guy in the suit walked away from the little knot of men in coveralls.

"They don't know a thing," said Ripper. "They go far away every day at quitting time, and there's trucks and people in and out of here unchecked. Thing about computers is they don't care about what they don't know about. No curiosity at all."

"So why you don't arrest them, the Messmer place," said Du Pré.

"Well," said Harvey, "see, we need warrants, stuff like that, and to get a warrant, you have to have a *reason*. We know exactly what they are doing up there. But we haven't got one damn shred of evidence."

"I miss Shannon Smiley," said Ripper. "Goes and dies on us just like that. I bet we go into that ranch, we find her face in a jar on the kitchen table."

Du Pré grunted.

"Okay," he said, "so why are these guys crawling all over this fertilizer place for?"

"We get criticized all the time for being arrogant pricks," said Ripper, "so, well, we just felt generous, shared our information with local law enforcement. Past that, we have nothing to do with this at all. My, my, that cop just fell off the tank, there. Hope he's all right."

"So why are you here," said Du Pré, "now?"

"I can't tell you that," said Harvey. "We . . . we're acting on a tip."

"Christ," said Ripper, looking disgusted, "you're gonna lie to the man, do a little better. You're supposed to be *teaching* me."

"Ineducable little monster," said Harvey. "You're a lost generation."

"What worries us," said Ripper, watching the police carry the man who had fallen away, "is that some mysterious citizen is whacking out bad folks so quick we feel jealous. Violating their civil rights, you know, cutting them in half with shotguns and skinning their faces off—cute, that, real cute, and what we like to do, see, is catch one of 'em and offer them a new life in exchange for a whole lot of information."

"We have had zip by way of these bastards doing that," said Harvey.

"Harvey," said Ripper, "there is a horrible vigilante out there! He's doing our job better than we can! We even know who he is!

202

And here we sit watching local law enforcement injure themselves crawling over a pile of *artificial shit!* It's come to this! *Artificial shit!*"

"So you arrest that Jerry Jacquot," said Du Pré.

"Tell you what," said Harvey, "you call ol' Jer' there and ask him to come on in and confess all and I will just do that. Or you could."

Du Pré looked off toward the Wolf Mountains, a faint blue hump on the horizon.

"These closed corporations," said Harvey, "you know, the thugs at the Messmer place, the rich thugs at the Martin ranch, very hard to get into those places."

"Not true," said Ripper. "I can ring up Queen Morgan, her of the Air and Darkness, and get a dinner invite just like that."

"Won't do no good," said Harvey.

"Harv," said Ripper, "you're too narrow. It would do a great deal of good. The food there is excellent."

"That Messmer place wants to ship horses tomorrow," said Du Pré.

Harvey looked at him.

"Why don't you tell me these things?" he said.

"You don't ask," said Du Pré.

"Harv," said Ripper, "Du Pré scares them, makes them mad, you know, they sure as hell aren't gonna be shipping a slab of crank out tomorrow stuck inside a bale of hay."

"Maybe they're getting bolder," said Harvey. "Or maybe they just want to kill Du Pré here."

"He needs an assistant," said Ripper.

"Jesus," said Du Pré.

"I got boots, I got a hat, I got a big belt buckle. Says Harley-Davidson but ain't it the thought that counts?"

"It could work," said Harvey. "Could make them very nervous."

"Jesus," said Du Pré.

"I like it, I liiiiikkkkke it," said Ripper.

"Maybe," said Harvey, "it's the fart starts the avalanche."

"Let's go to the saloon," said Ripper, "and I'll hang out, play pool, work on my drawl and bad jokes."

"Won't help," said Harvey.

"Blend right in," said Ripper.

Du Pré switched to drive and he turned and drove out to the highway and he headed west.

In two minutes he was doing a hundred and twenty.

"YYYEEEEEEEEHHHAAAAAAAAAAAAAAAH!" screamed Ripper.

Harvey pulled out his 9mm. He pointed it in the general direction of the engine compartment.

"You slow the hell down," he yelled, "or I shoot your damn horse."

Du Pré pulled his foot off the accelerator.

They drove back to Toussaint at a stately fifty-five.

Du Pré turned in and he parked at the bar.

Ripper got out. He went over to the government sedan and took a big nylon suitcase out and went on inside.

"He's a good kid," said Harvey. "Long as I can keep him out of headquarters he'll have a job. Got no sense. Could care less a superior has more rank. Insolent, insubordinate, and he don't like pompous fools."

Du Pré nodded.

They went on in.

Ripper had disappeared.

Benny Klein was sitting at the bar talking to Susan. She was at her beadwork again.

Du Pré went behind the bar and gave himself a drink before he got a soda for Harvey.

"I'll have some whiskey in this," said Harvey. "I'm off duty."

Du Pré poured out some soda and added whiskey.

"I got to go over to Cooper," said Benny. "Velma just called."

Du Pré nodded.

"Somebody stole one of them old buffalo rifles," said Benny. "A gosh-darned .45-120. Weighs twenty pounds."

Du Pré nodded.

The big buffalo guns could throw a six-hundred-grain bullet a mile, accurately.

Ripper came out of the men's john.

He had on faded denims and worn cowboy boots.

Ripper slouched up to Du Pré.

"Guddamned government," he said. "I seen one a them black helicopters out to ole Bud's place. Probably got the Tri Lateral Commission in it."

❧ CHAPTER 36 ❧

H im out in the shed," said Jacqueline. "Him outside, we think maybe like some sun on his feathers, skunk wander by, that damn owl get him. You know skunk, blow stink all over. Owl, him in shed till he smell some better."

"You don't feed him enough cats?" said Du Pré.

"Owls got own ideas," said Jacqueline. "Maybe that skunk, he smell good to that owl."

"Stinky owl, stinky owl, stinky owl," sang Alcide.

"Bullfit the owl," said Pallas. "Me, I want to talk about horth. Thaddle. I eat my vegetables."

Du Pré looked at the little faces ranged down the long trestle table that sat near the feeder ditch, only a couple of feet wide and a foot deep, that went past the backyard of Jacqueline's house.

Big enough for a little one to drown in, though. A female Labrador named Puff had the job of seeing that no one fell in and stayed there. She was very good at it.

"Yah, Puff," said Du Pré. He scratched the big black dog's ears. She limped when she walked. She'd been caught in a trap and lost part of her right front foot, and so she couldn't hunt except from a blind.

"You put your vegetables, a bag, feed them to Puff," said Du Pré.

"Alcide," said Pallas, "I kill you tonight. Wait till you thleeping good."

Du Pré looked at the tiny little girl.

"How come you can say Al-seed, can't say sleep?" he said.

"Don't know," said Pallas, "but it don't got nothing to do my horth."

"You are too small," said Du Pré.

Pallas looked at her grandfather for a long time.

"I don't want to *eat* the horth," she said finally. "I want to *ride* the horth. What how big I am got to do with it?"

"You," said Du Pré, "you are a lawyer you get big."

"That what it take, get a horth, I be a lawyer now," said Pallas.

"Me, I give up," said Du Pré.

"Papa," said Jacqueline, "you give up long time ago."

The children suddenly scattered from the table like a school of frightened fish. Two tiny boys fell to wrestling and Pallas chased Alcide with murder in her tiny little heart.

"How much longer these guards they are here, Papa," said Jacqueline. "I am scared some."

Du Pré shook his head.

"Ver' bad people," said Du Pré. "I don't know, how long."

"Long time there is none of this here, Papa," said Jacqueline.

Du Pré nodded.

Place don't change much, a hundred years, then it change plenty.

The back door opened. Raymond stood there on his crutches. He carefully moved down the steps.

At the bottom he lost his balance for a moment and then he got it back.

"We go, dance tonight," said Jacqueline.

"I am ready," said Raymond. He grinned. His white even teeth shone.

Du Pré moved so he could sit by Jacqueline.

"How is the owl," said Raymond, "him smelling better?"

"Not so good," said Jacqueline. "You want to give that owl bath, you have a good time, there."

An owl's talons would go through a human's wrist like hot needles through lard.

Raymond looked off toward the shed where the owl was locked up.

"I think I hear something there," he said.

Du Pré got up and he went to the shed and he looked through the grimy window. He couldn't see the owl for the boxes and workbenches and junk.

He opened the door, a little jammed from the hinges stretching.

The owl was in the middle of the floor.

He was standing triumphantly on a big dead bull snake.

His talons were sunk in the snake's brain and throat.

Du Pré sighed.

The bull snake was an old friend who kept the place free of rattlesnakes.

Him lunch now.

Du Pré went back to the trestle table.

"Him kill the bull snake," said Du Pré.

"Damn," said Raymond, "who eat them rattlesnake now?"

"I ask Papa how much longer those guards are here," said Jacqueline.

Du Pré sighed.

Me, if I had told that Harvey about that damn sick coyote with the cold burn on him foot, they would be gone now, but I don't think to.

When I tell that Harvey he blow up, call me a fool, say, that would be enough, a warrant.

"Well," said Du Pré, "I thank you for the dinner. I go play now, I am going to Messmer's tomorrow, they are shipping horses."

"You are careful, Papa," said Jacqueline.

Alcide came around the corner of the house. He was scratched and bruised and mournful-looking.

Pallas had finally caught up with him.

Du Pré laughed.

He got in his old cruiser and backed out to the country road and drove off to the Toussaint Saloon.

A cousin from Manitoba had been down visiting family in Billings and had wanted to play some music. He was a drummer. Played the flat-hand drum. Two crossed sticks and a withe circled and a skin over it, put on raw and wet and dried in the sun.

The drummer played the drum with a double-ended stick, one that had a knot of wood on one end and a gourd filled with some lead shot, not many, on the other.

My cousin Nepthele, play real good, I have not played with him maybe fifteen years. Twenty? Drives the big trucks, Canada.

Him call the bar, Susan say, sure he is here, you play for us, I pay you good.

Nepthele was sitting at the bar talking and laughing with Susan Klein and Bart. He was older and fatter than he had been the last time that Du Pré had seen him.

Du Pré looked a while at Bart.

"Bart," he said, "you are older and fatter than the last time me I look at you."

"Huh?" said Bart.

"My cousin is giving me a nice hello," said Nepthele.

"I am supposed to say you are younger, much better looking?" said Du Pré.

"Yes," said Nepthele, "I turn time backward. Louis said . . ."

They spoke for some time about the relatives they both had scattered across Canada and the U.S.

One hot-tempered cousin was in prison for shooting his wife.

"Canadians ver' mean to you, shoot your wife," said Nepthele.

"Well," said Susan Klein, "I should hope so."

"It is that Amelia he is married to?" asked Du Pré.

Nepthele nodded.

"Him need to shoot her," said Du Pré.

"Oh," said Susan Klein.

"She is pret' mean," said Du Pré. "Once she run off with this guy, gone six months, show up again, not a word. She do that."

"She is giving him children that are not his," said Nepthele.

"Men are never absolutely certain their children are theirs," said Susan Klein.

Nepthele looked at Susan Klein.

"You know this dangerous woman, long time?" he said. He grinned. He was missing some front teeth.

"Sheriff's wife," said Du Pré.

Nepthele nodded.

"She own this bar, him the Sheriff, they got the whole county," he said.

"Nobody fart here they don't want them to," said Du Pré.

"Hah," said Susan Klein.

Nepthele had some more of his beer.

"Keep hearing stories, you," he said.

Du Pré nodded.

"All good ones, though," said Nepthele.

Bart laughed silently.

Nepthele nodded and headed toward the john.

"What is this all about?" said Bart, watching him go.

Du Pré shrugged.

Cousin from Canada I have not seen fifteen years shows up.

Play a little music.

Du Pré went out on the front porch to smoke a cigarette.

Nepthele came out. He slapped Du Pré on the shoulder and

went down the steps and over to his car, parked across the street. He opened the trunk and he took out a package wrapped in brown paper and brought it to Du Pré.

Du Pré opened it.

A soft leather shirt, chamois, fringed and quilled and beaded. Madelaine.

"She say she miss you," said Nepthele. "She will come back soon."

Du Pré turned and looked at the Wolf Mountains.

He nodded.

✤ CHAPTER 37 ✤

Du Pré and Nepthele started playing music at nine. It was Thursday night, usually a slow one at the Toussaint Saloon. But the few people there called people who called people and by ten there were a hundred of Du Pré's friends and neighbors sitting at the tables or standing at the bar.

It was a night for the old music. No sound system, just the fiddle and the drum.

A couple of ranch couples who had some Métis blood came to the dance floor and they did the old dances, the clogs, heel-and-toe, staying in one spot while their feet spanked the old wooden floor.

The chamois shirt that Du Pré had on was hot, even though the big room wasn't terribly crowded. Sweat ran into his eyes and blurred them.

Nepthele was possessed. His drumming was polyrhythmic, a backbeat winding through the slaps and shushing rattles of the double stick, the knob and gourd. Sometimes he would stomp with his boot heel, another punctuation.

When that crowd is happy you go on with them, Catfoot had said, like you don't leave a woman who is breathing like that.

Nepthele stopped drumming but his boot heel went on thumping, and then he sang one long note and broke and the same note again and Du Pré nodded and he fiddled the Dance over the Water song.

It was many songs, a digest of a music that was already old when the Romans marched into the peninsula of Brittany.

Catfoot had played this only when he was very drunk. Only when he was drunk, Catfoot said, could this music come out of his bones.

Du Pré had his eyes shut against the stinging salt of his sweat. He flew along above the drums, Nepthele played a lot of different drums with one old worn badger skin stretched on chokecherry and birch.

Shot in the gourd, wood to the hide, the leather heel on the floor.

Then someone joined with them, a reedy deep wood tone, a melody turning within itself like smoke on a damp day. The player held the notes droning and then supply changed them, like a magician pulling coins and cards and scarves from empty air.

Du Pré stopped and wiped his eyes with his bow hand and he looked toward the droning woodwind.

Jerry Jacquot was standing by the little stage, off to the side, blowing into a snaking tube of brass that rose up out of a polished rosewood instrument thick as a piece of stove wood and nearly three feet long. There were brass keys on the side and both of Jerry's hands were hanging over the front, fingers stabbing at the brass keys or covering ports arranged in no good order down the gleaming wood. A bag was clamped under Jerry's left arm, a black ebony tube rose toward his mouth out of it, and from time to time Jerry would blow quickly and the bag would fill, and then he would return to the odd silver mouthpiece on the brass tube and his cheeks would bulge again.

Du Pré had never seen any instrument that looked like this.

Jerry's eyes were closed, the notes and drones spilled out to gather with Nepthele's many drums.

Ever' old, Du Pré thought, this is ver' old.

This songs, Catfoot would say, leaning forward on the kitchen chair, drunk and red-faced and slow everywhere but his fingers, this songs they come on them little fishing boats them French, English, Irish people sail over here long damn time before that Columbus come screw everything up. The people they sing this music, play it, they dance, stone huts, the shingle on the beach, the little decks, the shore here, dance on a hide pegged to the ground, the forest.

Man won't marry a woman can't dance.

She won't marry a man can't dance.

This songs, said Catfoot, his eyes closing, the bow sliding on the strings.

Songs of people running from bad times, go somewhere else, live a life. We go all the way across the ocean, but we don't want be famous, so we don't tell no one, next person come you do that him want taxes.

This songs, said Catfoot.

Du Pré nodded to the music as Nepthele and Jerry questioned and answered each other.

You know this?

I know that.

You know this?

I know that.

Du Pré took another break. He wrapped a kerchief around his head to catch the sweat and he knotted it behind his neck and he picked his fiddle back up.

Jerry stopped but he did not open his eyes, he swayed a little to the music.

He was dressed in faded jeans and a worn flannel shirt, dark green with big brass buttons, and low shoes like laced loafers. His hands were at rest, his fingers slightly bent, a musician's curve to them, power resting quietly.

Du Pré stared at him. He looked like what he was, a rich college boy, even his casual clothes were expensive.

Du Pré pulled Nepthele along behind him until they were doing a river-running song, the paddles dipping and the muscles straining to keep the big freighter canoe making way as it shot down the white water.

Broach to, it is lost, lose the kettles, guns, the bales of furs, the trade beads we can buy off war parties with, getting back to the factory where our women are chewing good buffalo neck hide to make those moccasin soles, so their men have good moccasins for the next long trip.

Down the water, down the water, death is wet and white.

Jerry didn't join in. He stood quite still now, not a muscle moving anywhere, the bag under his arm flaccid, his fingers standing well back from the keys and ports.

Du Pré finished the song abruptly, the canoe had slid into the calm water below the falls.

He looked around the room.

People were sitting stunned, still lost in the land the music had taken them to.

Nepthele put his drum and stick on top of the old upright piano on the stage. Du Pré tucked his fiddle in the case.

Jerry Jacquot was still standing with his eyes closed.

Paul Martin came out of the dim alcove in the far corner and walked to Jerry and touched him on the arm.

Jerry nodded and his eyes opened and he was awake.

Du Pré looked at him.

"Pret' good music," he said.

"What is that instrument there?" said Nepthele.

.

Jerry looked down at the strange thick wooden tube hanging from a strap over his left shoulder.

"I don't know," he said. "I haven't been able to find anyone who does, either."

"Damn old bagpipe," said Nepthele.

"Well," said Jerry, "it has a drone bag, of course, but it's keyed. It takes a reed in five places. It has a tube of brass worming around in it, and another of wood."

"Where you find it?" said Du Pré.

"Montréal," said Jerry. "A pawnshop. Been there for years in the window. It wasn't much. I bought it and went looking for someone to play it. But I couldn't find anyone. Finally I found an old pipemaker who did what he could, but even he had never seen or heard of anything like it. I did find a drawing in one of the Verendraye papers of an instrument like it, but just the drawing."

"Where you learn your music?" said Du Pré.

Jerry shrugged.

"Folklore collections," he said. "Canada is thorough about those."

"You are from Canada?"

Jerry looked at him.

"No," he said, "I'm American. But we had cousins, and so forth, in Montréal. I went there a lot."

"He would try and play this thing in our rooms," said Paul Martin. "His housemates nearly killed him."

Verendraye, Du Pré thought, they come maybe to Montana, 1740, first white men to write about it. They don't know where they are, but they write about it like they do.

Du Pré had a drink and then another. Jerry kept his strange instrument hanging from his shoulder.

The next set Jerry stood quietly for several songs.

Then Du Pré began the Song of Genevette.

Thrown away by her white husband. Albert Messmer, she pulls the sled with her babies in it through the snow, to the Métis camp, they save the babies but Genevette her feet and hands turn black. She dies of the blood poisoning.

Jerry played again.

The notes were sad beyond the telling and the drone was sorrow deep as a winter that would never end in the heart.

When the last note died away Du Pré looked at Jerry Jacquot, his eyes closed.

That is who you are, then.

Yes.

✦ CHAPTER 38 ✦

"I have heard all of them damn jokes they got twice," said Madelaine.

Du Pré grunted.

My woman she is bored at that Turtle Mountain.

"So I come home," she said. "Ride down with that Bassman, you play some music. They got good fiddlers here, but not like my Du Pré."

"Good," said Du Pré.

"Eh?" said Madelaine. "You are not worried?"

Du Pré grunted. He hated the telephone.

"We maybe see you day after tomorrow," said Madelaine. "I come home before you start skinning grandbabies."

Du Pré laughed.

"Pallas she is breaking my balls," he said.

"Pallas break anybody's balls," said Madelaine. "She remind me of that Maria."

Du Pré laughed.

"Them TV set," he said.

When Maria was four she took a great dislike to a mean man on TV who had a show with little kids on it that he used and hated. He smiled too much. Maria paid careful attention that fall to Du Pré, especially when Du Pré took his shotgun out and went to shoot pheasants. She asked grave innocent questions about where the shells went, how the gun opened, what was that little button there?

"Safety," Du Pré had said. "You got to move it like this, gun don't go off, safety is like *that*."

Du Pré was out in the yard in back doing a chore when the shotgun went off in the house, boom, and the TV tube blew up, boom.

Jacqueline was crying, scared out of her wits.

Maria was quietly sweeping up little bits of glass. The wing chair was overturned and the shotgun was sitting on it.

"You!" Du Pré had said to his tiny daughter, furious and scared.

"Don't like that man," said Maria. "Him gone now."

"TV set is gone, too!" said Du Pré.

Maria had looked up at her furious father.

"You tell us them good stories," she said. "Better than that TV."

Du Pré went off to comfort the wailing Jacqueline.

After Jacqueline had quit blubbering and Du Pré had her drinking some fruit juice, he went back to little Maria, still cleaning up the slaughtered TV.

"Me," he said, "I spank you now."

My guts are churning, Du Pré thought, me, I don't know what to do.

Maria had looked way, way up at her father.

"No," she said.

"Why I not spank you?" Du Pré said.

"No," said Maria. She went back to sweeping up, since the subject was now talked to death and resolved to her satisfaction.

Du Pré tried to regain the upper hand but suddenly he realized he had never had it. He threw his hands to the sky and helped clean up.

Bart was out working on some problem Popsicle had. The gigantic dragline sat in gleaming vile green splendor under a metal half-shed, a roof and partial walls hanging down far enough so that snow would not gather on it. Popsicle was carefully tended and all dings and scratches were soothed and painted immediately.

Du Pré went out of the house and across the rutted ranchyard to Bart, who was up on a ladder doing something to some hydraulic lines.

"Madelaine is coming back," he said.

Bart looked down. He nodded.

"Kelleher is selling out," he said. "Shipping all of the horses today. Whatever they were up to, they gave up on. They're just businessmen."

"They are bastards," said Du Pré.

"Just businessmen," said Bart.

"Businessmen they don't murder people," said Du Pré.

Bart looked down on Du Pré.

"Pass me," he said, "that other socket, there. Please."

All the horses.

Du Pré heard a car turn in far down the long drive.

Harvey and Ripper.

They drove slowly up to the shed. Harvey was slumped down over the wheel, laughing.

Ripper jumped out. He was wearing a long, bright pink frock coat and a tall gray top hat, black pants and running shoes. There was a big white card stuck in the narrow silk band on the top hat.

PRESS.

Said the card.

Du Pré remembered where he'd seen a hat like that. In a children's book he had read to Jacqueline and Maria when they were small. *Alice in Wonderland*. The Mad Hatter wore one like Ripper's hat. The card had said 10/6.

"Harvey was good enough to drive me out here," said Ripper. "I quit first thing this morning. Handed him my resignation, on a napkin. Told him to shove his goddamned FBI up his ass. But I like Harvey, so I made sure the paper was soft."

"Christ," said Bart.

"I am a journalist writing a piece on . . . on . . . what's that title every hack uses? 'Cowboy Meets Cappuccino.' 'The New West!' Meet cattle brand inspector Gabriel Du Pré, a certified member of an oppressed minority group and therefore worthy of my good ink."

Harvey was waving a napkin.

"I am free of this little bastard," he said. "Praise the Lord."

"Harvey told me there was racism in America. Told me at breakfast," said Ripper, "and I was *shocked. Shocked!*"

Harvey was carefully folding the napkin.

"You are going, the Messmers, with me?" said Du Pré.

"Sure am," said Ripper. "Have it on good authority late at night those folks are mean to ducks. There's an environmental angle, you know."

Ripper pulled a camera bag out of the tan government sedan he and Harvey had driven up in. He carried it over to Du Pré's old cruiser.

"Gabriel," said Bart, "if you take that madman out there, and you get yourself and hopefully him shot, I'd have to testify you both deserved it."

Ripper dashed back. He whipped out a notebook and he addressed one of the posts that held up the roof over Popsicle.

"Mr. Rancher, sir," said Ripper, "do you see any reason why you and your ugly wife and horrible offspring and land maggots—those awful cows you've been raising here for six generations—should not be removed at once so that the buffalo may roam again?"

Ripper listened intently as the post spoke to him.

"Thank you, sir," he said. "I'll twist your words like any good journalist."

Bart had gotten down from the ladder.

"It could work," said Du Pré.

"It better work," said Ripper. "We don't have anything else."

"Why you don't just go in there, search it?" asked Du Pré.

"Probable cause," said Harvey.

"You got a guy in there?"

"Left a couple days ago," said Harvey. "They got him jammed up day and night. Can't get anything out. I hope he just leaves. They're on to him."

Du Pré thought of the two hands. Okay.

"What they'll do," said Harvey, "is sell out to another corporation they own. They can take years if they want to. We can't watch them here for years."

Du Pré nodded. Me, neither.

"It stinks," said Harvey.

Du Pré nodded.

"They never quit," said Harvey, "and this has been like trying to nail water to the wall."

"Why they kill that Shannon Smiley," said Du Pré, "she does good work for them?"

"That did not make any sense," said Harvey.

"Cut people's faces off," said Du Pré.

Harvey looked at him.

"Long time since we did that, Du Pré," he said, "but I hadn't thought of that."

Blackfeet catch some guy on their hunting grounds, scouting the buffalo for his people, they cut his face off him and then they dump him near his people's camp. See, this is what happens, you try to steal our buffalo. You wander forever after death and you got no face and nobody knows you.

"Jesus Christ," said Harvey.

Métis do that, too. You talking to the Blackfeet, you got to speak their language. We are just as bad as anybody we have to be.

Them Blackfeet don't give us our hunting grounds.

They got meat to get before the winter, too.

"Gabriel," said Harvey.

Du Pré was looking off toward the Wolf Mountains.

He shrugged.

"Long time gone," he said.

"Dooooo Prayyyyyyyy!" shrieked Ripper, "there's a story out there!"

"Okay," said Du Pré, "we go now."

❖ CHAPTER 39 ❖

A man Du Pré had never seen before was at the gate that guarded the drive to the Messmer Ranch compound. He was a heavy, middle-aged man with dead eyes, dressed in a baggy pair of slacks and a windbreaker even though the day was hot. He glanced into the car and he waved Du Pré on and Du Pré saw him talking into a radio when he glanced at the rearview mirror.

There were eight huge horse trailers and double-tired pickups parked waiting to load the stock.

"I'll pop out when you've warmed up the crowd," said Ripper, from under a blanket next to a couple of coolers in the back seat.

Du Pré parked and he got out and he pulled his leather case with the forms after him. He put the strap over his shoulder and he stood and stretched.

The horses had all been hazed into a big round corral and they moved nervously in little groups.

A dozen men stood by the horse trailers, quiet, not talking.

Du Pré walked over to them. They were Westerners and the trailers and trucks had license plates from several states. Idaho, Wyoming, Utah, Colorado, Nevada, California, New Mexico.

You can auction stock over the telephone but it still has to be inspected before it is shipped.

The buyers nodded when they saw Du Pré's badge.

"We don't take so long," said Du Pré.

Kelleher was walking toward the little group.

224

"Well," he said, cheerily, "these gentlemen need to be on their way."

"Load them up," said Du Pré, "I check the trailers, you don't got to run them past me, I have seen them before."

Kelleher had a clipboard filled with bills of sale.

In half an hour the horses were loaded and Du Pré began inspecting and signing off. He matched bills of sale to shipping chits. Everything was in order. He could glance at a horse he had seen before and remember the brand or brands. Some had three or four.

As Du Pré ripped the forms off the board and passed them out, the buyers started up their huge pickups and left, wallowing down the drive to the county road.

The horses were gone, every one of them.

Neither Roddy nor Bill were there.

"Well," said Kelleher, smiling, "I guess that's it . . ."

Du Pré saw a feather, a small cloud, something white moving off at the far corner of his vision in his right eye.

He turned his head and he looked.

Puff of white smoke.

The boom of the rifle began and then there was a wet ripping sound and Kelleher flew fifteen feet and slammed into the last horse trailer.

Du Pré hit the ground.

He looked back toward the puff of white smoke.

That goddamned buffalo rifle.

"Yeeeehaaaaaaaaaaaah!" screamed Ripper, flying past Du Pré toward Kelleher, whose face was contorted and unbelieving. Blood was seeping and welling from his abdomen.

"Where's Roddy?!" screamed Ripper, putting his hands on Kelleher's gut. "Tell me and I will save your life."

Kelleher said something that Du Pré couldn't hear.

"I lied, you fat fuck," said Ripper, getting up. "Do die already."

Ripper pulled out a 9mm pistol and he went to the saddle bays in the front of the horse trailer and he shot the lock off and jerked the door open.

A man with his head wrapped in duct tape was jammed in there, his wrists in handcuffs.

"Du Pré!" yelled Ripper. "Get some help, get an ambulance, move the fuck will ya!"

Du Pré ran to the cruiser and he grabbed the radio and switched it on. The dispatcher took his message and rang off.

Du Pré walked back to Ripper, who had the man from the saddle bay out on the ground. He was carefully cutting away the gray tape from the mouth and nose.

"Breathe, damn you," he said.

The man wiggled a couple of fingers.

"Good," said Ripper. "Now this is gonna hurt so good."

Ripper tore away tape. There were gauze pads over the man's eyes.

"Get some whiskey will you," said Ripper. He was cutting away with his pocketknife, and pulling firmly. The man's face was emerging, all bruised and abraded. The lips looked like chunks of raw steak.

Ripper cut the last of the helmet of tape away, slicing hair, like he was skinning the man's head.

A little blood ran from the top of one ear.

Ripper cut the tape that bound knees and ankles and he pulled it free. He pulled a ring of keys from his pocket and he bent over the handcuffs.

Du Pré heard them snap open.

"Just lie back now, good buddy," said Ripper.

Ripper reached up and Du Pré put the fifth of whiskey in his hand.

Ripper poured some into the man's mouth.

The battered man choked and spluttered.

Du Pré got a bottle of water from the cooler that had been on top of Ripper.

Kelleher was still breathing in little pants but his eyes were fixed.

Six-hundred-grain bullet make a big damn mess.

Ripper's Mad Hatter hat was crown down on the ground and the card had fallen out.

Du Pré heard a siren faint and far off.

"Be just a minute," said Ripper to the battered man. "We'll get you taken care of here."

Du Pré looked out toward the road.

The guard and the SUV he had been driving were gone.

"I maybe go and see about that rifle," said Du Pré.

"Sure," said Ripper.

Du Pré went through the fence and on across the big pasture toward the rock a mile away where the puff of smoke had suddenly appeared. There were greasy black wisps rising from behind the rock.

Du Pré stopped and rolled a smoke and then went on. The tracks of horses and their turds were thick on the ground.

The rock was an ordinary chunk of limestone that rose at a gentle angle from the hillside and dropped off abruptly, a sheer gray face twenty feet high.

Something red on a stick.

A feather waving in the wind.

Du Pré laughed. He walked up the path that led around the rock and up and he stood for a moment looking.

The huge .45-120 buffalo rifle was out near the edge, the two brass-mounted cane sticks the barrel rested on holding it up. The stock was set carefully on a small rock covered with a wisp of grass. The narrow brass telescope gleamed in the sun, the first such sight ever made.

Du Pré picked up the rifle and racked the lever forward.

A single huge brass shell flipped out. There was nothing else in the magazine.

Two more of the big cartridges were set upright on a flat rock.

There was a single tussock of grass on the rock's lip.

A spear was stuck in it, point down, and one crimson eagle feather waved from the shaft.

Du Pré laughed.

He walked to a small wad of black leaking smudges of smelly smoke bitter to the nose.

Burning rubber.

A little wad of latex. That used to be rubber gloves.

Du Pré found the moccasin tracks leading back to the skein of brushy watercourses that lay crazily all over the apron of hills leaned up against the mountains.

Hard to find a man in there if you were looking.

Du Pré looked back toward the ranch buildings.

Flashing blue lights.

Harvey Weasel Fat aka Wallace talking to the Mad Hatter.

Ripper was jumping up and down.

Du Pré sat down on a rock beside the buffalo rifle.

He rolled a smoke.

He laughed.

A cop car had made it out into the pasture and was roaring toward him.

Du Pré stood up.

He turned around.

A couple of miles away to the west a canyon cut out of the flank of the Wolf Mountains, and a chunk of yellow limestone sat on each side of the cut the creek had made through living rock.

A man was standing on one of them.

He had on a bright red shirt and tawny pants.

No hat.

Du Pré waved.

The man stood, feet apart.

Then he raised both arms to the sky.

Then he turned and trotted away into the dark forest.

✦ CHAPTER 40 ✦

"You, Harvey," said Madelaine, "you look, someone piss in your pop. So you got a bunch of dead bad guys, crank lab all busted up. It is not like your dog died."

Harvey Weasel Fat aka Wallace narrowed his eyes.

"Nobody piss, my pop," said Harvey. "Just some asshole, blow away a son of a bitch I am trying to bust for years. It is called murder. Very embarrassing, it happens while you stand there, your handcuffs the one hand, your dick in the other. Us FBI, we got to write reports. I don't like, begin, 'There I stood, dick in my ear . . .'"

"Your bosses, they don't like poetry?" said Madelaine.

"My bosses, don't like us look like idiots," said Harvey. "This guy, whips in and out of anywhere he want, smoke, night, like a Crow steal horses."

Du Pré laughed, shaking, silently.

Them Crow steal horses off a fire engine, it is headed out.

Lots of cowboys, pushing cattle, sleep, wake up, nighthawk is out cold. Then they get to pick out, cow they want to ride. Crow never hurt the cowboys. Why? say the Crow, they are dead they cannot bring us more horses. Us, Crow, we like them cowboy fine.

"Worst thing," said Harvey, "is we don't have any idea who this guy is. People like these assholes, they kill each other all the time. But it is not them. We talk to everybody, they say, shit, we don't got any idea. It is not us."

Snitches, Du Pré thought, got nothing to sell the cops.

The Toussaint Saloon was filling up with people, dressed for a night out.

A fourteen-year-old girl, daughter of a rancher, wandered up to Du Pré, blushing.

She carried an expensive tape recorder, the size of a briefcase.

"Mr. Du Pré?" she said, "could I . . ."

Du Pré nodded and he got up and he went over to the little stage with her and he helped her set up the tape recorder, plugging it right in to the sound system so there wouldn't be so much distortion.

The girl played fiddle very well and wanted to get better. She was too shy to play in public yet, but her father had taped her and brought a sample.

Du Pré had listened to the tape. She was very good, except when she tried too hard and her fingers stumbled over each other.

"She wants lessons from you," the rancher had said. "I can pay . . ."

"She is fine," said Du Pré. "Music it is for us all, she keep after it, she play when I am dead. But that music it goes on. She is doing fine. She don't need lessons."

The rancher nodded.

"Maybe a little better violin, though," said Du Pré.

So Du Pré called a fiddle seller in Canada and found a good one for not too much money.

The girl came every time Du Pré played, except on school nights, and sometimes even then.

"You maybe come play a couple songs soon," Du Pré said, when they had the tape recorder set up.

"Oh no," the girl said, "I'm not good enough yet."

"You got to be good enough sometime," said Du Pré. "Music it is not complete there are not a lot of people dancing to it."

"Sometime," said the girl. She looked petrified with fright.

"Now time," said Du Pré, "You got your fiddle, I see you practicing outside, I am taking a break. You come on up, play, I am behind you, you get real scared, fall, I catch you."

The girl swallowed hard.

"Okay," she said, in a very small voice.

She went off to her parents and talked to them and her parents lighted up. They shone, proud of her.

Du Pré went back to Harvey and Madelaine.

"Harvey he is whining," said Madelaine. "He says it is not fair, send good FBI agents to this place. Local people make fun of them, shoot their bad guys, big joke."

Du Pré snorted.

"Gabriel," said Harvey, "you could help me here."

Du Pré drank his drink, rolled a cigarette, lit it.

"Harvey," he said, "I help you all that I can but you got to go away first. Maybe you go tonight. Take your friends. It is not for you this."

"We'll be back," said Harvey.

Du Pré shrugged.

They had a couple more drinks.

Agent Ripper came in, dressed in jogging clothes. He was running sweat and breathing deep. He coughed.

"Is there a no-smoking area?" he said.

"You can not smoke anywhere you want to," said Madelaine, "you pick anyplace you want, I come take the ashtray away."

Ripper pulled up a chair and he sat down.

"I need a veggie burger," he said.

"Great," said Madelaine. "You go and gather your roots, bark, I fry them up for you."

"Organic beer?" said Ripper.

Madelaine smiled brilliantly at him.

"Everything we got," she said, "organic."

She went off and got drinks and a huge schooner of beer and a pop for Harvey.

"We make this out of goat piss," said Madelaine, setting the schooner in front of Ripper. "Goats are very organic."

Ripper drained it in one long swallow.

Bassman came in the back door and in a second his latest burlap blonde followed. This one had a ring in her left eyebrow and others in other places.

Du Pré walked over to the young fiddler. She was white-faced and determined. Her parents were being calm for her.

"We do three," said Du Pré, "then I call you up."

"Okay," said the girl. She smiled bravely.

Bassman ran his fingers up and down the fretboard and the bass rumbled, a soft sliding low staccato.

Du Pré got his fiddle out and he tuned it, only one string a little flat. He remembered bumping the peg casing it the last time.

They began. Du Pré played a couple of reels and then a slow one, about slow water and black trees down to it and loneliness.

"Okay," he said, "we got this new fiddler she is plenty good you be quiet for her, she is nice enough play for you." He waved to the girl. She came forward, stumbling a little when her boot toe hit a chair leg.

Du Pré held out a hand for her and helped her up.

"Okay," he said. "We stand sideways, you look at me."

The girl nodded.

Du Pré started a jig, an uncomplicated one. The girl nodded for a few measures and then she closed her eyes and she bowed the fiddle.

Du Pré muted his fiddle with his chin and he nodded at the girl.

Bassman's bass runs kept the rhythm and color steady.

The girl breathed deeply once and she took off.

Du Pré nodded. The girl wasn't improvising, just trying to do a good job. She did, only faltering once toward the end.

Du Pré stood back and he lifted his fiddle and bow high.

The crowd clapped for the girl.

Du Pré led her up to a run again and let her fly. She did this perfectly.

Then there was a long droning note, like a bagpipe but more mellow and full.

Du Pré looked out into the room.

Jerry Jacquot was standing there, the strange beautiful instrument in his hands, his eyes closed and his mouth and cheeks full of air.

He was dressed in the soft smoked buckskins of the Métis of the Plains, a linen shirt, a small round hat on his head with one single eagle feather hanging from the brim in back.

"Oooooh," said the girl. She backed away.

Jerry played a melody.

Du Pré gave it back to him in little chopped pieces.

Jerry played a long droning note, one that twisted and rose.

Du Pré followed, wind to the bow.

Jerry walked forward, his feet in the high moccasins. A knife in a beaded sheath was stuck in his Red River sash.

When Jerry got to the stage he stepped up and he turned and he began to sing.

The Song of Genevette.

His Coyote French was the dialect of Manitoba.

Genevette pulling her babies through the snow. She dies. But then Jerry began to sing verses that Du Pré had never heard.

My sons will have sons and they too, Genevette had sung as she died.

My daughters will have sons.

234

They will bring these sons to my grave and sing my song.

One day one will hear it and he will return.

He will be a warrior, who will fight alone.

He will walk through time like it is only snow falling.

He will find the tracks of my sled, carrying my babies through the snow.

He will follow them back.

❧ CHAPTER 41 ❧

Mr. Du Pré," said Morgan Martin, "have you breakfasted?"

Du Pré shrugged. He had played music until two and slept a few hours and then he drove to the Martin Ranch. Following Jerry Jacquot in one of the ranch trucks.

Jerry was off packing his bags.

Morgan Martin left Du Pré sitting in one of the big leather armchairs in the vaulted living room. She was whistling.

Du Pré got up and he went over to a bundle of African spears and a shield that were hanging on the high log wall next to a huge pair of elephant tusks. The spears were black-pointed, with thin silver edges. He put a finger on them and he felt the lacquer.

He yawned.

Morgan Martin returned with a tray. She set it down.

Poached eggs. Bacon. A muffin. Coffee. Glass of water. And a big bowl of fresh raspberries, some red and some black.

"The black ones are Persian," said Morgan Martin. "Lovely flavor though. We have contrived to grow them most of the winter in the greenhouse, and con them into producing in the fall, too."

Du Pré ate. The raspberries were delicious, lightly sauced with red sugar and vermouth.

He finished and he drank coffee.

"The tusks," said Morgan Martin, "were got by my great-uncle. I think he shot one of everything, including a Zulu or two. Some

236

family legend about being attacked in camp by robbers. Don't know if it's true. But the tusks definitely came from an elephant."

Du Pré nodded.

Piss on my boots, this one.

Jerry Jacquot came in. He was dressed in slacks and deck shoes and a soft chamois shirt.

"It's all out by the car," he said.

Du Pré got up.

"Well," said Morgan, kissing Jerry on the cheek, "do come back."

Du Pré looked away. Morgan Martin, really pissing, my boots.

Then Morgan Martin swept off down a hall. It was a family that never said good-bye.

Jerry Jacquot shrugged.

They walked out to Du Pré's old cruiser. Du Pré and Jerry put the bags in the back seat and they got in and Du Pré turned around and drove down the ranch road toward the highway.

"Couple places I would like to stop on the way," said Jerry.

Du Pré nodded.

Yes.

He shot along past the Wolf Mountains on his right and down to the north-south highway. He turned.

The road south went straight as a taut string over the rolling High Plains, down toward the Missouri and then the Yellowstone.

Jerry Jacquot pointed off to the east a little.

"The trail went along that line of little buttes," he said, "down about nine miles it comes close to the road."

Yes, Du Pré thought, it is where the snow it will be lightest, where the wind clears the ground and the grass, the buffalo go along that, too.

Du Pré got up to a hundred and ten and they shot along, slowing coming up hills and when the road was clear miles ahead speeding back up, passing a couple of big rigs laboring at less than half their speed.

The deep line of the Missouri slashed across the land ahead.

"Over there," said Jerry, pointing.

A dirt road left the highway, winding over the slabbed hills to a small canyon and then following the little creek down toward the river.

Du Pré had never been to the place before.

Good place to camp, though, had water and cover and wood, plums would have grown in the draw, good for making pemmican, and there were good places for riflemen to guard the paths.

The Métis would have liked this place, near to the buffalo trail, and pretty safe. Beyond for a couple days' travel by cart it was very dangerous, the broken ground the Sioux and Blackfeet liked to hide in, wait, attack.

They got out of the car and Jerry Jacquot ran light as a deer along the trail back up the side of the hill to a rock.

Du Pré followed slowly. He came up to Jerry, who was standing on the rock, a low one only a couple feet higher than the grass.

"Genevette," said Du Pré, "is something to you?"

"Just a song," said Jerry Jacquot.

Lying son of a bitch.

"Du Pré," said Jerry, "you know, I don't mind telling you a story if it is left here for the wind."

Du Pré nodded.

"My mother and Janet Messmer were roommates in college," said Jerry, "And Janet was my godmother. When she was murdered my mother was so very sad. She wept for weeks. One night I heard her talking to my dad, and she said Janet had been killed by her brother and that she had always been afraid of him and now it had happened."

Du Pré rolled a cigarette.

"I was only eight when that happened," said Jerry, "but I remembered it, and then my mother died of cancer, and . . . I went to school, met Paul, started to play music. I studied engineering, aerospace, actually, and I was digging through the collection and the school of music when I saw the drawing of the strange instrument. It was called a genevette. I did a little fiddling, and in time got the proportions right—the drawing was freehand and all off. The acoustics are complicated. I think the genevette was invented by some genius who saw a bagpipe once and just remembered a little of it."

Du Pré nodded. The rest of this story I should know now.

"Then I found the Song of Genevette and I had to dig to find the history. She was my great-great-great grandmother. The Métis, they sing it up in Manitoba. I thought we were just French and English, but in time I got it right."

Du Pré nodded.

"What a terrible way to treat anyone," said Jerry, "let alone the mother of your children. Albert Messmer drove Genevette out and then she came here. Where the plums are by the muddy water. She must have died right here, Du Pré."

Du Pré ran through the verses in his head.

Maybe.

"The yellow scraper rock," said Jerry, "across the muddy water."

Du Pré looked over the Missouri. There was a rock formation on the far side shaped like a scraper, the stone tool used to clean flesh from hides.

"So Genevette was buried here," said Jerry, "where she could see the sun come up."

Du Pré nodded.

Jerry Jacquot jumped down from the rock and he ran on up the trail that wound up to the flat-topped hill.

Du Pré followed.

Jerry was kneeling down by a small fissure water was opening in the rock and earth.

He pointed to the rock.

Black on dark gray-yellow.

The Métis would have built a fire to thaw the earth to let the grave be dug.

Du Pré looked around.

There were other places but this was as good as any.

The wind was picking up and it wailed over the rocks, wailed like Métis women grieving in dreams.

Jerry Jacquot knelt and he took a rosary from his pocket and he prayed quietly for a while.

Then he took a wooden pennywhistle from inside his jacket and he began to play.

The Song of Genevette.

All of the story.

Du Pré counted off the eleven verses.

Jerry Jacquot played three more.

He got up.

"Make tobacco?" said Jerry.

Du Pré offered his pouch. Jerry took a pinch and he scattered it in the little wind while his lips moved.

Du Pré looked down the Missouri, the brown roiling river, the yellow-white walls of the canyon.

Jerry began to walk back down to the cruiser.

Du Pré followed, whistling.

Me, I ask him the three verses I don't know, Du Pré thought.

He don't tell me, I can write them anyway.

✦ CHAPTER 42 ✦

Madelaine put herself up on her elbow and she looked down at Du Pré and she grinned.

"You miss me some, eh?" she said.

Du Pré nodded.

"Okay," she said. "You maybe fucked enough I would like to go, a walk, get some of them salmonberries, dye some quills."

Du Pré laughed.

"You gone a long time," he said.

"Dance with them Turtle Mountain people," said Madelaine, "but I want, be here with you, doing what we just done."

They got up and they dressed and they went out to Du Pré's old cruiser and they got in and he drove off up toward the foothills of the Wolf Mountains.

They passed Benetsee's place, but there were no signs that anyone was there.

"That old fart," said Madelaine, "him gone too much. I give him some hell he get back here, that Pelon, too."

Du Pré turned off on a ranch road and he came up to a gate and he got out and opened it and Madelaine drove the car through and he shut the gate and he got back in and they bumped up toward a little canyon with the right water and sun for salmonberries.

Madelaine had brought a plastic bucket and a bag and a pair of cutters with her. She handed the bag and cutters to Du Pré.

"Them stalks need to be dead but the bark still on," she said.

They walked up a path and into the cool of the narrow canyon. A tiny creek rushed out of it, and trout no more than four inches long darted back and forth in the little pools.

The salmonberries grew in small stands on flat ground.

"Bear been here," said Madelaine.

Salmonberries were a bear favorite, though pretty tasteless.

Madelaine began to pick the berries and Du Pré cut the shoots and trimmed them and he put them in the bag, in pieces four inches long.

They moved slowly up the creek.

There was a loud WHOOF and the bear crashed off up the mountain.

"He could stay here, eat berries," said Madelaine.

The bear changed direction suddenly and started running, crashing into trees in its panic.

Somebody coming down the trail, Du Pré thought.

"So that Jerry Jacquot is a bardache," said Madelaine. "Me, I got a couple uncles bardaches, too. They are nice men, very kind, good people."

Du Pré stopped and he rolled a cigarette.

"How long after you know it is him you don't stop him?" said Madelaine. "You know that Harvey he gets mad with you, says someday he is putting you in prison, just can't figure out how."

Du Pré laughed.

"Him got his troubles," said Du Pré. "Him bitch to you, eh?"

"Harvey," said Madelaine, "him better off retired. I tell him, Harvey, you live, that whiteside bullshit you don't got, take it so seriously."

"Song wasn't done," said Du Pré.

Madelaine stopped.

"That is ver' good, Du Pré," she said. "Maybe you are not

hopeless like ever'body say. Me, I say, that Du Pré is just a stupid man, you know how they are, but him try so hard."

Du Pré nodded.

Okay.

"Harvey is maybe retiring, a year," said Madelaine. "He says he will never come here again. Send somebody named Ripper."

Du Pré nodded.

"Who is this Ripper?" said Madelaine.

"Crazy man," said Du Pré. "You, you like him."

"Yes," said Madelaine. "Crazy men I like."

Du Pré heard a squirrel chirr a hundred feet up the mountain. He stopped and stared. Nothing moved.

"Roll me my smoke," said Benetsee.

Somebody fell over something up the hill and they cursed.

"Pelon, him city boy," said Benetsee, "fall over ever'thing. Maybe he die falling over, I get another, cut sweat lodge wood."

Du Pré laughed.

The old man hopped across the tiny creek. His ragged clothes were black with dirt and his running shoes were scuffed and stained.

Du Pré rolled Benetsee a thick smoke and he lit it and he passed it to the old man.

"Shit!" yelled Pelon. He was closer.

"Fall in creek," said Benetsee.

Pelon came out of the trees, dripping and holding his elbow.

"Get lost, the graveyard," said Benetsee. "It is next, the church, he don't see it, though."

"Fuck!" said Pelon.

The young man was limping.

Madelaine looked at Benetsee and Pelon.

"Jesus," she said, "you look starved but not dead. You come on I feed you. And you, old man, I get you new clothes, too. Shoes."

243

Benetsee nodded.

"Salmonberries," he said, "don't taste like much."

"Good for dyeing things," said Madelaine.

Benetsee nodded.

They all walked down to the cruiser and got in and Du Pré drove back down to Madelaine's. They went in and Madelaine began to pull things out of the refrigerator and she found a loaf of bread and a big crock of butter and she pointed to Du Pré.

"We eat outside," said Madelaine.

Benetsee grabbed the butter crock.

"Not you," said Madelaine. "You, you take a bath. Jesus, you stink. You give me them old clothes we burn them I got new ones."

Benetsee meekly went off toward the bathroom.

"You next," said Madelaine to Pelon, who was still rubbing his arm. "He walk you all to Canada?"

Pelon nodded.

Madelaine went off toward the bathroom with a big plastic bag and she came back with it filled and she put it outside and went off to the back room and she carried some clothes and new running shoes back with her and she went to the bathroom and opened the door and tossed them in.

"You wash them feet three, four times, old man," said Madelaine.

Du Pré laughed.

He went out into the yard and he sat at the picnic table and he smoked. Benetsee came out looking clean, his clothes fitting fair around him.

"Bardache, him," said Benetsee, "him Genevette's."

Du Pré looked at Benetsee.

"Genevette she is dead a hundred years before he is born," said Du Pré.

"Him long son," said Benetsee.

Long Son.

Genevette she reach down, sure enough.

"Bad people," said Benetsee, "I see them one night. That Porterfield she tell me about this long ago."

Du Pré looked at him.

"Had these pictures," he said. "Me, I look at them, say this is not over. She says she wants to see it done."

Du Pré nodded.

Funny woman. But you don't like your history you can come here and find some that you do like, make it your own.

"You got wine, a thirsty old man," said Benetsee.

He still had dirt in the wrinkles of his face, but Madelaine would get it.

No escape.

Du Pré went into the house and he found a jug of horrible screw-top wine, bubbling with sweet gas, tasting of bubble gum and lemon peel. He filled a big jar and he brought it back out, carrying the jug in his other hand.

Benetsee drank it all down. He held out the jar and Du Pré filled it up.

"I know you, younger, you don't listen to them songs," said Benetsee.

Du Pré laughed.

"Older is better, some things," said Benetsee.

No shit, Du Pré thought, I be as much an asshole, you.

Madelaine came out with a soapy washrag. She marched up to the old man and she scrubbed his face hard.

She told him to go and rinse with the hose.

Benetsee went off. Du Pré laughed.

He looked off toward the Wolf Mountains, rising blue and gray and white to the north.

Snow melt up there, some goes to Red River.

Song, a long time gone, comes here.

Du Pré rolled a cigarette and lit it and then drew in a deep drag.

He blew it out.

Long Son.

Yah.